PINK
Sneakers

Dolores Yergeau

PINK Sneakers

DOLORES YERGEAU

BELLASTORIA PRESS
Stories from the Heart

ISBN: 978-1-942209652

Pink Sneakers

Copyright © 2019 by Dolores Yergeau

BELLASTORIA PRESS
P.O. Box 60341
Longmeadow, Massachusetts 01116

To my dear father,
whose storytelling during my childhood
brought me great joy and instilled a love of literature
I would like to share.

Chapter 1

For a brief moment, when the first light of morning broke through the darkness, the sun's rays crept along the ocean's surface. It began at the edge of the horizon until the golden light sparkled and overwhelmed: a signal which started the new day. Eileen watched motionless, sole witness to this glorious sight. As she gazed at the waves rolling in, she couldn't help but think that it looked the same as it had so many years ago. But no, not everything was the same.

She was leaning across a large rock to steady her arms as she took a series of shots with her camera. She knew that she would find at least one picture to develop into a painting. Satisfied, she put away her camera, and set out for her walk.

As the sea breeze moved her hair, she breathed deeply, bringing its salty coolness into her body, uniting her more strongly with her surroundings. Her spirits rose with the shrill sounds of gulls overhead and the crashing waves around her. She felt the powerful pull of the tide as the sand was sucked out from beneath her bare feet. Sandpipers scurried about on slender legs as she approached their feeding spot. The summer sun's rays heated pools of water as she walked gingerly along with renewed energy. This, she felt, was a spiritual awakening.

Eileen smiled as she let memories seep back into her mind: memories which were bittersweet, which rushed back and forth like the tide, whose waves might be welcome or too strong to accept.

Dan was gone now, yet here she felt his presence so strongly that she glanced at the sand as if expecting to see his footprints beside her. How many times had they walked this beach with her hand locked in his, confirming a oneness that was theirs alone? They had a special bond and a perfect partnership that they had so enjoyed. *How lucky can you get?*

"Face it, Eileen," she reminded herself. "Dan has been dead over two years now and it is about time that you got on with your life. You can't live on dreams that vanish in the wind."

Having completed her walk, she headed towards the lone bench by the dunes where sat a sole occupant, a gentleman busy writing or drawing in a notebook. She wondered if he was an artist, too, and perhaps trying to catch the same scene that she found so appealing. She always used that bench when putting on her sneakers, and although she didn't want to disturb his concentration, her waiting sneakers were beside the bench.

Just as she drew near, she noticed a small terrier under the bench. He had stretched his leash far enough to reach her sneakers and had just closed his mouth on one of them, when she yelled out, "Your dog has my sneaker!" Immediately, the man dropped his pencil and pad and reached under the bench to retrieve the sneaker from his dog.

"Skipper, what are you trying to do? Get me in trouble?" he said to his dog. He handed Eileen her sneaker, which showed no damage thanks to the quick action of the gentleman. "I apologize for my delinquent dog. Skipper likes to pick out his own toys. Sorry about that!"

"Well, I'd say that Skipper has good taste, so don't worry about that," Eileen reassured him.

"You know, I'm here most mornings and I've seen your pink sneakers, so you would think I would have known they would be of interest to Skipper." Changing the subject, he asked, "You're a photographer, aren't you? I've watched you planning the best light and angle with each shot."

"Actually, I'm an artist. I wasn't aware that I was being watched. This is the first time I've seen you here."

"That's because I'm usually gone before you finish your walk. I find inspiration for the short stories that I like to write whenever I come here."

At that point, he stood up and said, "Let me introduce myself. I'm Eric, and you've already met Skipper." Hearing his name, Skipper responded by coming to his master.
"He knows at this time, I usually unleash him and bring out his ball so he can show me just how fast he can retrieve it. Isn't that right, Skipper?" Eric then threw a ball a good distance from where they were, and, true to his reputation, Skipper went out and back in a flash with his ball in his mouth. Eileen was impressed. Eric handed her the ball and she tossed it. Skipper bounded after the ball, picking up speed as he grew nearer.

Then, suddenly, he let out a yelp and returned with his front paw up in the air. Eric ran to him and removed a sharp piece of broken glass from his bloody paw. When Eileen saw the steady stream of blood coming from the wound, she removed her sneaker shoe lace and tied it above the paw.

Eric picked up the whining dog in his arms. "This calls for a trip to the veterinarian's. Since I walked to the beach, may I ask you for a ride to my cottage to get my car?"

"I don't think we have time for that. How about I drive you both to the vet's? That wound needs immediate attention."

While his dog was being treated, Eric explained how he ended up owning his pet. He used to go out often in his friend Jim's boat. Skipper was Jim's dog. Unfortunately, Jim died suddenly and he left Eric both his boat and his dog. Eric paused and said, "Now, I can't imagine my life without my buddy, Skipper."

"Do you still take your boat out often?"

"As often as the weather permits. It's a small boat, but it serves my needs. And if you want to see Skipper's tail wag, all you have to do is say, 'Boat!'"

Eileen smiled as she pictured the two of them off for an afternoon sail.

After Skipper was treated, Eileen drove a grateful Eric to his cottage. Eileen held the door open for Eric to carry Skipper inside and then gently place him in his doggy bed. Her shoe lace was returned and she sat to lace up her pink sneaker. She smiled at Eric when he said, "This has been a very trying day. Please let me make you a cup of coffee while we catch our breaths. You realize I don't even know your name?"

"Eileen Egan. And, yes, I'll accept that cup of coffee. My heart went out to poor little Skipper. He was trying to be so brave. It's good news that he should be all healed up in ten days. I'm just happy that I was there to help when it was needed."

Eric was still shaken after seeing his beloved dog suffer because of someone's careless disposal. Now, he wanted to know more about this kind lady.

"This cottage is my refuge from the often hectic academic life that I lead as a college English professor. It is so peaceful here—a perfect fit for Skipper and me. Now, what is your story? Are you just vacationing, or do you live here?"

"This is where I live now. I used to have an apartment in New York with my husband. Once he died, it lost its appeal and our summer cottage became my permanent home and my place of business. This works well for me."

"So you sell your paintings right from your house?"

"No. I ship them to my agent in New York and she handles everything for me. My clients contact her. Now, I only have to go to New York for any showings that she books for me. I'm happy to split the profits with her and let her worry about the marketing part of this business. That leaves me with the enjoyable part– just painting."

"Are all your painting subjects about the ocean?"

"No. Mostly about nature. I have very few still life paintings in my collection."

"The reason I ask, is I think that there is a scene that you might find picture worthy. You see, I go horseback riding once a week. Towards the end of the trail, I stop to admire the view. Do you think that you might be interested in joining me on my next visit there? I know a gentle horse there, if you're nervous about riding."

Eileen thought a moment and said, "You know, I might take you up on that! I'm always looking for fresh ideas. But I'm not sure about getting on a horse, since my last experience was when I was in my teens. Hey, what the heck, let's give it a try!"

Eric felt that maybe, in this small way, he could repay her for her help. They set a time to meet again and Eileen left for home.

Once at the cottage, she started a pot of coffee and put some cereal and fruit in a bowl. As she poured the milk over the cereal, her thoughts drifted back over the whole morning scene. Up until they sat for coffee, Eileen hadn't thought much about Eric because she was too upset about Skipper. Now in her own home, she seemed to get a clearer picture of him. He really was a good-looking man. It was evident that he was intelligent, too. Yes, he was a pleasant person to talk with, she concluded. Eileen was forty-eight years old and she guessed he was about her age, or a little older. She recalled his startling green eyes that looked straight at her as they spoke. And that full head of reddish, brown hair added to his good looks. *I hope that I am not making a mistake accepting his invitation!*

She headed for her studio. On her easel was a large canvas with a rough sketch of the seaside. Taped above it was a photo taken to refresh her memory of that scene. She put on her smock and arranged oil paints on a pallet. The color of the sky captured in the photo was appealing, so aloud she said, "Cerulean with just a touch of cobalt and some white should do it." Taking a large brush, she mixed the paints and watched the changing colors before her. How she enjoyed looking at colors. They always cheered her up when her mood was off.

"Great, just what I was looking for," she said with a satisfied smile. And for the next couple of hours Eileen was lost in creating a favorite scene that she had visited many times in the summer. She stopped and studied what she had painted so far and ended up saying, "It's coming along."

After lunch, she put on her garden gloves, put her tools in a straw basket, and brought out a foam rubber pad to kneel on. Heading for her little garden, Eileen stopped to admire the profusion of color from her budding flowers. Again, the mixture of so many different colors warmed her heart. "My beauties!" she said. Then she knelt on her pad and began pulling the few weeds that had sprung up to compete with her lovely flowers. Gardening helped erase the troubling thoughts that were trying to surface in her mind. She could hear his voice just as plain as if she had a recording of their brief conversation. Still, she thought, "What do I really know about the man?"

After gardening, she took out the novel she'd started the day before, picking up the story where she'd left off. It was an interesting read, but her mind kept drifting. She felt a need to move about, which led to her taking out the vacuum cleaner and freshening up the cottage. It did help burn away some of that pent-up energy.

Next, she took out a cookbook and challenged herself to whip up something delicious for supper. But she soon lost interest in that.

Still feeling restless, she decided to freshen up a bit with a cooling shower and a shampoo. She fussed with her hair, letting the blond highlights take on a new sheen as she brushed and watched the loose curls form softly so that her short haircut framed her oval face in a flattering style. She was five-foot six, and all her walks and healthy eating habits had paid off to her benefit, leaving her long legs muscular and shapely.

That night, she lay in bed wondering if she even remembered how to get on a horse, never mind, riding one. "Oh well, I guess I'll find out soon enough."

Meanwhile, Eric was having similar feelings. Once she had left, he sat there going over everything she had said. He shuddered to think of what would have happened to Skipper if she hadn't offered her assistance. Eric was surprised that he was so taken with someone he had just met.

Not wanting to leave Skipper alone too long, he decided to shorten his daily bike ride. He was a little over six feet tall with strong, long legs, used to bicycling many miles a day. Eric's bike riding was his favorite mode of transportation. His bike was a source of pride and he took good care of it so that the salt air didn't rust the bright blue paint. His Bridgestone RB-1 was a racing bike. Eric preferred the steel frame over some of the newer, lighter materials.

Now, as he started to peddle along, he wondered how meeting this woman had managed to lift his spirits after such a short encounter. He suddenly was aware of the silly grin he wore and the increase in speed as he headed back home.

He pulled up to his cottage, put away his bike, and went inside happily humming. He gave Skipper a treat, pleased that the little dog seemed comfortable. After putting on the coffee, he grabbed a doughnut from the bakery bag.

Eric's table served as his desk, too. As a result, it was cluttered with books and papers. Being an English professor, he made sure that he was never very far from his work. Brushing aside the papers, he made room for his laptop and breakfast. While eating, he looked over the few paragraphs he had written in the morning. He saw the need for a few changes, but, all and all, it wasn't bad. It was amazing that he could think straight when his thoughts were filled with that enchanting woman.

No alarm was necessary the next morning. He was too excited to sleep any longer. He could see that the fog had rolled in. It crossed his mind to bring a thermos of coffee for both of them. But then, he thought that would be a bit too presumptuous and certainly would scare her off. Maybe at some later date it would be a good idea.

"What if I asked her to give a woman's viewpoint on the character I'm writing about? That way, she would know there's no woman in my life right now or I would have asked her instead of Eileen." He laughed to himself.

He spent extra time shaving and primping before the mirror. He slapped on some aftershave lotion, spent more time cleaning his teeth than usual and looked for a better coordinated outfit to wear. The little pluses count.

In her own cottage, Eileen also woke a little early and noticed the heavy fog outside and hoped that wouldn't call for a change in plans. Once up, she put on her hooded fleece jacket to ward off the chill in the air and left for the beach.

Wanting to arrive before Eric, she began her walk earlier than usual. The fog blocked the view of the ocean until she came almost upon it. The water felt too cold at first but as she progressed along the way, she gradually became adjusted to the temperature.

"I'm not going to look back. I wouldn't be able to see the bench anyway in this fog. When it lifts, I will just look straight ahead," she promised. She began to walk faster.

The fog lifted just about when she reached her turnaround point. She took a deep breath and turned. The bench was very far away and too tiny to make out if someone was on it. Realizing that she was hurrying, she deliberately slowed her step. As she continued on, the bench came into view, and there he sat.

"Oh, he's looking this way. Why isn't he writing?" She warned herself not to look in his direction. She became self-conscious and started up towards the bench, keeping her gaze down as if watching for broken shells to be avoided. When she finally looked up, she was relieved to see him busy writing.

"Good morning, Eric. And how is the patient doing today?" she greeted him. He looked up as if surprised and responded with, "Ah, the early morning walker! Well, you can see for yourself." He nodded toward the back of the bench and there was Skipper in his doggy bed, with a light blanket wrapped around him. Eileen went to him and petted his head while talking to him. His wagging tail was a welcome response.

She picked up her sneakers and sat a little closer to Eric this time. This gave him encouragement to further the conversation. "Not a good day to subject my laptop to all this dampness, so my notebook will have to do."

"Well, I must say that cameras have certainly improved. I love my digital camera and cart it around to capture some of my favorite scenes. Once home, I can use my printer to have the photo ready for me to use in a painting. So much easier than dragging my paints and equipment down here."

"And I am enjoying my summer months just writing for fun. I guess that we're both lucky that we can make a living doing what we like to do."

"My sentiments exactly," chimed in Eileen.

Eric had tactfully edged a little closer to Eileen and asked, "Tell me, do you ever take private commissions, or do all your paintings go to New York?"

"I've painted for a few people who've seen my work and have asked for something specific, but I don't encourage it. I'm just busy enough to enjoy my work. To take on more might be overwhelming. Why do you ask?"

"I feel that my cottage is rather plain and I've wanted to brighten it up, but never got around to it. I think a nice oil painting would perk up a rather dull room. Are you interested at all?"

"You have no idea what my paintings look like," she laughed, "but if you want to take a chance, I'll give it a try." At that point, she took out her camera and showed him some old photos that she had used for paintings. He was impressed with what he saw.

"And may I ask what you charge for a painting?"

Most of her paintings sold for well over a thousand in New York. Her agent would figure in her cut, which was quite high. Since no agent would be involved, Eileen could lower the price.

"It depends on the size. But it would probably be in the five or six hundred dollar range. You can look at my work and talk about it at my office. Should we plan tomorrow at one?"

"That would be fine with me, Eileen."

It sounded nice hearing him say her name.

Eileen checked her pockets to see if any of her business cards were there. She found one and gave it to him with a little hesitation. Everything seemed to be moving so fast that it made her uncomfortable. Ready to leave, she stood and said, "Okay, then. I'll see you tomorrow at one. Enjoy the rest of your day."

Eileen was home but a few hours when the phone rang. It was Eric.

"I know I'm to see you tomorrow, but Skipper would like to go boating and forget about his accident and he was wondering if you would like to join us. There is usually a gathering at the shore to view the sunset, but we prefer a private viewing from our boat."

It was a hot day and the thought of a cool breeze and pleasant sightseeing was very appealing. Having good company would be a bonus, so she accepted the invitation.

Late afternoon, they took out the boat for an early ride before the sunset. As Eric increased the speed, Skipper held his head high, embracing the wind and loving every minute of it. The thrill of the moment was not lost on his master as he headed away from the shore.

When they finally slowed down, Eileen asked the obvious question, "You really love it out here, don't you?"

His big grin said it all. "It's hard to put into words exactly what I am feeling. I'm surrounded by the ocean and as it moves my boat, I feel joined with its life. It's an awesome feeling! But the light is fading so we need to get back and drop anchor."

Once anchored, they could see families gathered on the shore, seated on their blankets. There were parked cars in the lot above, where the occupants were protected from the cool dampness of the air as they watched the sky in anticipation. The nightly show would soon begin with or without an audience. Those waiting knew they would not be disappointed. There is something special about a summer's day drawing to a close and signaling the sun's spectacular descent.

They watched in awe from their little boat as the brightness of the day dimmed and introduced a new palette of color across the waiting sky. Sparkles of gold dressed the parade of waves as they marched in a rhythmic flow to their foamy end. Vermillion streaks competed with yellow hues extending their dazzling display. A kaleidoscope of changing colors was mirrored in the sea below, allowing it to join in the parting presentation. Reds became orange and yellow melded into gold against the azure sky.

They had watched in silence until Eric whispered, "Now, watch as the sun shines with a burst of brilliant, blazing color, to remind us, for one final time, just who really is the prima donna of the evening sunset." Eric's words gave extra meaning to what they now viewed. It was an experience that Eileen would never forget whenever she viewed future sunsets.

Chapter 2

Roxann Rehan, a twenty-year-old college student going into her second year, knew what she had to do if she wanted to graduate with her class. She started plotting the easiest way to accomplish that goal.

Her wealthy parents had insisted she attend college, even though she had barely earned enough credits for her high school graduation. What they had in mind was a big-league university; however, they reluctantly agreed that Roxy could attend a small Maine community college with the hope that she would buckle down and be able to transfer to somewhere a little more prestigious.

As a freshman, Roxy discovered that her lazy work habits had continued to hold her back—habits she didn't intend to change if she didn't have to. After giving all this much thought, Roxy concluded that if she could raise her English grade, it would do the trick. Professor Ames would not be a pushover. He seemed too wrapped up in his English department to pay attention to a flirty student.

Roxy had to change her plans when she heard that her professor would not be teaching any summer classes and, in fact, would be away at his beach cottage all season long. With a little help from her friend in the school office, she was able to find out where his cottage was located. Next on the agenda, was a phone call back home.

Being an only child had its advantages. She set the direction of her own life. Once through with this college, her goal was to travel throughout Europe and end up working as a recreation director at a resort owned by one of her father's friends. She figured that this was an awesome way to meet a wealthy prospect.

Anne Rehan loved her daughter, but was aware of her spoiled, manipulating nature. When she heard Roxy's voice dripping with honey, her first thought was, *So, what is she up to now?*

"What's up, Rox?"

"Hey, Mom. I have a great idea that I want to run by you. I know that you and Dad wanted me to take summer classes, but I did some figuring and it won't be necessary. I found out that my English professor will be at Breaker's Point, Maine, for the summer and maybe Daddy could convince him to tutor me for a few weeks. And just in case he is not interested, I am bringing up my books so that I can study without distractions. I'd like to stay at some all-inclusive place so that I can devote my full time to my studies. How's that sound to you?"

Anne knew that her fun-loving daughter wasn't going to spend her summer studying. Maybe Jack could make it worthwhile for the professor to give some private lessons and improve her grades. *I guess it would be worth a try. It certainly wasn't the worst idea that girl had come up with.*

With a resigned sigh, Anne answered, "Okay, Roxy, I'll tell Dad of your idea and see what he thinks. We'll get back to you."

"Cool! See ya." And with that she ended the call.

It took some convincing, but Anne was able to sway her husband that Roxy was sincere in her request. As promised, Roxy's dad phoned for reservations at the 5-star, Royal Haven

Inn. That was the easy part. Getting in touch with the professor proved a little more difficult.

The phone rarely rang at the cottage because so few knew his phone number and that is the way he wanted it to be. Eric was out on his porch reading a new novel he'd picked up the day before, when he heard the phone ringing. He went to the phone with his lemonade in his hand and noticed the ID showed the name Rehan. Eric cringed. Roxy was one of the worst pupils he had ever taught. When she showed up for class, if she showed up at all, she was always looking down at her cell phone. It was obvious that she wanted to be anywhere else than where she was. His thought was, "Now, why the heck is she phoning me here and how did she manage to get this number?" His "hello" wasn't a happy one.

"Professor Ames. Jack Rehan here. My daughter, Roxann is spending a good part of the summer in your area and I was wondering if you could tutor her for a few weeks?" He paused before saying, "You know I would make it worth your time."

You've got to be kidding! "I am aware of your daughter's need for extra schooling, Mr. Rehan, but I have never taught during the summer and don't intend to start now. The reason I come up here is to forget about teaching. You can understand that. Right?"

"Look, why don't you just name your price and your hours and we'll set it up."

"I don't think you heard me correctly, Mr. Rehan. This is not about money. It's about time. My time. And I don't wish to spend it teaching. There are other tutors who would gladly help her catch up."

Jack Rehan wasn't used to being refused. His money always sweetened his requests. "Tell you what, professor, why don't you give it some thought and I will get back to you."

Eric was having trouble controlling his temper. *No wonder Roxy was so pushy with her classmates.* "No need to phone back, Mr. Rehan, as I have already given you my answer." And with that, he hung up.

As her bright red Mercedes entered Breaker's Point, Roxy checked out the streets. When she finally arrived at the Royal Haven Inn, she smiled. It looked expensive, and it was. All meals were included, so that all she had to think about were her studies. Yeah, right!

After she registered and was shown her room, Roxy freshened up and put on a low cut, tangerine silk blouse and tight-fitting white jeans. Her shoes had heels high enough to add another two inches to her five-foot, six-inch frame. She knew that she had a great figure and she made sure that everyone else knew it, too. Her hair was dyed different colors and worn long and straight. She liked heavy makeup and lots of mascara to show off her large brown eyes.

She checked herself out in the mirror. "Watch out, 'cause here I come." And she headed for the downstairs bar.

Back at his cottage, Eric woke up to loud thunder and lightning. "Well, that rules out our meeting at the beach. Thank God, we'll see each other this afternoon." He ate breakfast earlier than usual and worked on his novel, which always made the time pass very quickly. His story was turning into a romance instead of a mystery. He'll just let it carry on through, he reasoned, as nothing was set in stone yet. He sat lost in his characters as the morning passed and the storm was long gone.

Lunch was simple for Eric and that suited him just fine. He usually read the morning newspaper while he ate his sandwich. He had checked out where Eileen lived and was pleased that it was close by. He didn't want to arrive too early and seem overly anxious to be with her, so he planned to make a point of being right on time.

His car pulled up to a pretty white cottage with green shutters. There were flower boxes loaded with colorful petunias spilling outside their boxes. In front were flowering hydrangea, lilacs, and honeysuckle against a trellis. Two round gardens held a variety of annuals with stones circling each garden. Yes, he expected her to live in just such a cottage. He rang the bell.

Eileen tried not to rush to the door after staring at the clock for so long. And as their eyes met, she felt her face redden in a blush. Eric grinned.

"Eileen, what a nice-looking place you have here. Do you do the yard work yourself?"

"It isn't work to me." She pointed to vases filled with freshly picked flowers. He followed her to her studio and was impressed by the paintings that were hung on the walls. Most were seascapes. The more he studied them, the more he liked what he saw. Actually, any one of them would be welcome in his place. Everything seemed to be neatly arranged. The clutter he expected just wasn't there. A rolling cart contained large jars of all size brushes. Small boxes on the shelves were labeled: acrylics, watercolors, pastels, etc. On the outside wall of the cart someone had made panels just the right size for her oil tubes. Each tube was labeled underneath. All the reds were side by side, as were the other colors. Since he noted that most of her work was in oils, he assumed she needed them right by her side to squeeze on her pallet. A closet door was opened enough so that Eric could see shelves filled with art books and canvases.

Eileen directed him to a table with two chairs. She sat down and Eric followed. "As you can see, I am a realistic painter. If you are after something more contemporary, I am afraid I can't help you."

"No, no. This is exactly what I had in mind. You see, I'd like a painting of the lone bench where I sit and write. You could take your camera there and capture it. I'd also ask you to place your pink sneakers beside the bench and paint them in your picture."

Eileen was speechless.

He saw her hesitation and quickly added, "That is unless you are uncomfortable with that?"

She smiled and said, "I'll see what I can do."

"I could give you a check now, if you wish. Whatever you decide will be fine with me." They agreed on a down payment and he gave her a check, looked at his watch like he had other errands to do and started for the door. He stopped midway and turned to her and said, "Eileen, how would you feel about having company on your morning walk?"

Hesitating, she said, "I am there very early, Eric. If you don't mind arriving a half hour earlier, I guess it would be fine by me." She still was uncertain about this idea.

The next morning, Eric didn't find it difficult to get up earlier. When he arrived at the beach, her car wasn't in the parking lot. That was good, as he didn't want her waiting for him. He walked slowly to the bench and noticed how bare the bench looked without those pink sneakers in the sand next to it.

It wasn't long before he heard her car and stood up to observe her approach. Walking towards him or away from him, she was a joy to watch. She looked up and smiled. She wore a lightweight jeans jacket and her white Capri pants. Her hair was free and blowing in the sea breeze.

She took off her sneakers, put a small hand towel inside one of them and placed them under the bench for later.

"I see you beat me here. We're the only ones here at this hour."

He kicked off his sandals and joined her as they headed toward the ocean. His blue jacket with the hood felt good as the breeze increased. They started along the shoreline and the pace they chose seemed just right for both of them.

He had to talk louder to be heard over the wind and waves. "There is so much life to an ocean, don't you think? It can appear calm and comfortable, and yet have a hidden undertow waiting to pull you under and out. It's always so full of surprises."

His hands were in his pockets, but that is not where he wanted them to be. He wished he could hold her small hand as they walked along.

Eileen stopped suddenly and bent down to pick up a treasure she had found. "Oh, look, Eric. I found a sand dollar!" She brushed it off and examined it before claiming, "It's perfect! Have you ever heard the legend of the sand dollar?"

That perked his interest as he let her know that was new to him.

"The story goes that in the center there is a star and around it is an Easter lily. The openings are said to represent the five wounds of Jesus. Once the sand dollar is broken, it's supposed to release the five doves of peace. On the reverse side is a design of the poinsettia, the Christmas flower. That's the legend, and some say finding a sand dollar will bring good luck. So today might be my lucky day."

"I like that, Eileen. Thanks for sharing."

A large gull was looking over the leftovers from the outgoing tide and made certain that he cleared the path before they got there. When they turned to head back, their walk was more comfortable because the wind was at their backs. They grew more accustomed to the icy water flowing over their bare feet or were they just numbed by it? When they reached the bench, they were ready to sit.

Eileen dried off her feet, put on her sneakers and sat back feeling content. Eric rested his long arms on the back of the bench, knowing that it was almost, but not quite, like putting his arm around her.

"Longfellow wrote of the sea's secret and said, 'Only those who brave its dangers comprehend its mystery!'"

"I like that, Eric. Can you remember any more of the poem?"

"It is called, *The Secret of the Sea.* I know it starts, 'Ah! What pleasant visions haunt me, as I gaze upon the sea! All the old romantic legends, all my dreams, come back to me.'"

"Longfellow knew how to touch the heart." It was easy to see that Longfellow was Eric's favorite poet.

Eileen was impressed and declared, "I will have to look that one up because it is so very beautiful. Can you recall the rest?"

"It's been awhile, Eileen. Let's see." He paused for a moment, then said,

> *Like the long waves on a sea-beach, where the sand as silver shines,*
>   *with a soft, monotonous cadence,*
> *Flow its unrhymed lyric lines.*

"The ending was especially moving," he concluded, and recited the closing lines.

> *Til my soul is full of longing, for the secret of the sea,*
> *And the heart of the great ocean,*
> *Sends a thrilling pulse through me.*

Eileen said nothing, just sat there letting his recitation sink in.

Eric said, "So many of the poets were enchanted by the sea. Have you ever read the sad poem that Tennyson wrote about the sea?"

"No. Do you remember it?"

Eric thought a minute and said,

> *Break, break, break,*
> *On thy cold gray stones, O Sea!*
> *And I would that my tongue could utter*
> *The thoughts that arise in me.*
>
> *O, well for the fisherman's boy*
> *That he shouts with his sister at play!*
> *O, well for the sailor lad,*
> *That he sings in his boat on the bay!*
>
> *And the stately ships go on*
> *To their haven under the hill;*
> *But O for the touch of a vanish'd hand*
> *And the sound of a voice that is still!*
>
> *Break, break, break*

At the foot of thy crags, O Sea!
But the tender grace of a day that is dead
Will never come back to me.

He ended with a sigh and Eileen joined him in thought.

"Oh, I didn't mean to treat you like a student in my English class. It's just that when I sit here looking at the sea, all these poems flood my mind. If I could bring my students here when we're studying these poems, it would be so much more meaningful."

"Both poems have their own appeal. Do you memorize many poems?"

"Not many, just favorites that I have read enough times that they stay with me. I wish my students could see for themselves what poetry has to offer them." He shrugged his shoulders. "As the old saying goes, 'You can lead a horse to water, but you can't make him drink'."

Eric switched his focus from the ocean to Eileen. "Well, I do go on, don't I?"

Eileen turned and looked at him with tenderness.

"I loved listening to you, Eric. As a child, my father used to recite poetry for no special reason. Not only from the works of well-known poets, but also from his own personal favorites. There was one that seemed to be directed at me and I believed it was a declaration of a father's love for his daughter. It was called, *Jennie Kissed Me*, by Leigh Hunt. I never tired of hearing it. I can try to remember it."

"Please do."

Jennie kissed me when we met; jumping from the chair she sat in.
Time, you thief who loves to get sweets into your lists, put that in!
Say I'm weary; say I'm sad; say that health and wealth have missed
    me; say I'm growing old – but add, Jennie kissed me.

It was still hard to recite that poem without feeling a tightening in her throat as thoughts of that dear man saying those words came back to her.

It was obvious her childhood story had made an impression on Eric.

"What a great way to express his feelings to his little girl. You were lucky. You know that?"

"Yes, I do know that. My sister and I both were certainly aware of his great love for us. We were fortunate in having such loving parents." On that happy note, Eileen stood up and Eric joined her in walking to the parking lot, where they reluctantly said their goodbyes.

Two days later, Eric picked her up to go horseback riding. His horse seemed to know him and he gave him a treat. Her horse was known as the gentle one. Eric helped her up and she nervously remarked, "I don't remember feeling this far off the ground when I was last in this position."

They continued on the trail. Eileen became more and more relaxed and they took their time enjoying the ride. She knew immediately when they came to the spot that Eric wanted to show her. The way the ground sloped, leading to a small lake, foliage, and peaceful quiet caused them to stop and dismount. Before she took out her camera, she paused and savored the view. As many times as Eric had been here, he never tired of the scene before him. Eileen took a few shots and then the two of them just sat in silence feeling the warmth of the sun.

Finally, they mounted their horses and started back to the barn. Half way back, a deer darted out of the woods, spooking Eileen's horse. He reared up, but Eileen held on tight. He then began to run, ignoring Eileen's pulling on the reins. All her riding confidence disappeared as she leaned forward to stay seated. Eric immediately signaled his horse to chase after the frightened horse. When he reached her, he was able to grab the rein and stop the run.

"Eileen, are you alright?"

"I am now. I thought for sure that I was going to be thrown. Thanks, Eric."

"It is so rare for that to happen. I am sorry it had to be with you."

Now that her horse was calm, she too, calmed down and continued their ride.

The next day, Eileen received a phone call from Eric. Riding together was still on his mind and he hoped they could do it again. For today, he had plans to visit an old cemetery and take pictures of some grave stones to present to his students as prompts for stories. He thought Eileen might like coming along.

"What a great idea, Eric! Yes, I would like to join you."

He took her to the oldest cemetery that he could find, and some stones were so old that you could hardly read them. Some specified that death was from drowning. That alone could be the start of an interesting story. One wonders if the person even knew how to swim? Perhaps it was a boating accident? The list could go on. He included those headstones in his shots.

"This one might make a good story, Eric!" She was looking at a weather-worn stone not quite upright. "He was born in Ireland in 1793 and died in Maine in 1869. Did he long to go back to his homeland, and was his decision the right one?" Another marker with a sad story said, "Child found in the river here. 1899."

They found many graves of children, which caused them to question what ended their young lives and caused such heartache to the parents.

They studied the different artwork engraved in the stones. There were poignant poems that touched their hearts and left them silent. Time passed, and they had no idea how long they had been there. But what they did know was that there were many stories that lay buried in the old cemetery.

On their drive home, they both thought about the people that once lived out their lives in this same area where they now live. It had been an interesting day.

The following week, the sun shone brightly and the weather report predicted a perfect beach day. Eric phoned and suggested that they have a late walk and enjoy a picnic lunch at the beach. Eileen liked the idea and packed a nice lunch in her picnic basket along with two glasses. Eric insisted on bringing a bottle of wine. The bench was occupied, so Eileen spread a blanket on the sand.

Families laughed at the water's edge. Children were busy with their pails of water making houses in the sand and jumping the waves as they went for refills. Eileen laughed when she noticed that Eric had brought along two pails and shovels.

"What have we here, Eric?"

"I have plans for after our lunch. We are going to make a beautiful castle together."

So after their tasty meal and flavorful wine, they filled their pails with water and poured it on the drier sand. Once it was just the right consistency, Eric gave all his attention to carrying out some plan that he had in his mind. Eileen was assigned the building of a wall that held in water for a mote, while Eric packed down the wet sand and shaped a large building. Turrets began to form under his strong hands and Eileen joined in with poking little windows and doors here and there. On their hands and knees, they delighted in seeing a plausible castle appear before them. A few families stopped to admire their work and Eric and Eileen stepped back for one final look of approval, and a few pictures, before leaving the area.

They both agreed to rebuild the castle before the summer ended.

As the weeks passed, they spent more and more time together. They extended a trip to the lighthouse by stopping first at a couple of antique stores. One shop in particular had many display tables, each representing a different dealer. The dealers were not present, only his or her wares. This allowed for a greater selection, which then could be paid for on the way out. Eileen spotted items that she remembered as a child. There were dolls, toys, and household things that are no longer in use. It was like going down memory lane for both of them. Eric got caught up in examining some old tools and wood carvings. Eileen chose a small colorful music box which showed six Rufous Hummingbirds feeding at different flower blossoms. She was always attracted to hummingbirds, so she picked up the small, round container and took the cover off, where she found a key. To her delight, it played a song that she often sang in her church choir, *Ode to Joy*. She decided she couldn't leave without her small treasure.

Eric found a wooden box that looked like a desk top from an old school house. It could fit on his lap and he could write on its slanted cover. When opened, it had plenty of room for his papers. This would be just perfect for his novel.

So after hours of poking, under, over and on the many display tables, they left happy with their selections.

When they arrived at the lighthouse, Eileen tried camera shots at different spots and angles. Then they sat on a bench and watched visitors scaling the slippery rocks for a closer look at the ocean.

From there, it was a short drive to a homemade ice cream store. With its many flavors, it attracted long lines outside. Eileen saw many delicious-sounding flavors, making it a problem to choose. She sampled one before picking two scoops. Eric knew what he wanted and had his in a waffle cone. Being a slow eater, Eileen had hers in a cup. They had their treats at an outdoor picnic table, watching families trying to hurry before the drippings spilled down their cones. With full bellies and smiles on their faces, they headed back home.

Chapter 3

Eileen was anxious to start on the preliminaries for Eric's painting. She went back to the beach mid-morning and found families on the beach with laughing children building castles with the wet sand. She was in luck, because the bench was empty and, fortunately, the position of the sun at this time of day afforded adequate lighting.

Placing her sneakers in their usual spot, she stepped back to judge her composition. She tried different distances, with a few so close that it filled the viewfinder. Next, she faced the bench for another angle, followed by a shot from the side that clearly made her sneakers the center of interest. Satisfied, she left for home.

At home she owned a laser printer, which would do for these tryout shots. Usually, Eileen had her photos professionally developed, but she was in a hurry to look over this unusual subject. Her printer was at work while she prepared a quick lunch, and then she ate while studying the results.

"I have a feeling as to which photo Eric will choose for his painting."

Eileen phoned Eric and asked if she could drop by to go over the photos. He quickly agreed. She let him know that there were a few chores she had to tend to first, but he could expect her to arrive sometime in the afternoon.

Eric couldn't be more delighted. He glanced around the place as if he was looking at it for the first time. Tearing off a few paper towels and dampening them, he proceeded to do a passable dusting which, for him, involved going around each object instead of lifting each one for a complete job.

He placed fresh towels in the bathroom, straightened pillows in the living room, and removed magazines from the coffee table.

And then the doorbell rang.

How could she be here this early? He wondered. He ran his fingers through his curly hair in what would have to do as a quick combing and, taking a deep breath, opened the door.

"Oh, God, NO!" He couldn't believe his eyes. There stood Roxy at her tawdry best. She wore a short, fire-engine red T-shirt. That, along with low-cut jeans shorts showing off her flat stomach with a diamond stud in her navel and a smiley, purple tattoo just below her navel.

She wore her hair pulled up with dyed streaks in it of different colors held up with a jeweled clip. Her pretty face was clowned up with the brightest of red lipstick and heavy, black liner around her eyes. Her highest stiletto heels completed the Roxy look.

After Eric recovered his voice, he angrily asked, "What the devil are you doing here?"

Roxy threw back her head, raised her eyebrows and strutted past Eric while chewing casually on her gum.

"Hey, Professor."

Feeling his blood pressure rising, Eric replied, "I made it very clear to your father that I have summers off. Period!"

Ignoring his remarks, Roxy checked out his kitchen. "Nice place ya got here. Bet it gets kind a lonely at night. Right?"

Eric pulled out a kitchen chair and told her to sit down. He sat and calmly explained that he had no intention of tutoring her, but, if she was serious about doing makeup work, he would give her an assignment.

"And what would that be?"

"I have a poetry book that you could borrow. I'll expect you to do a self-study. You are to write ten one-page essays on ten poems in my book. Once you hand it in, I'll tell you if you have made the grade. You do your part and I will do mine. Agreed?"

"Yeah, sure."

Eric swirled around and headed towards his bedroom. "I have a bookcase in my bedroom. Now, you wait right here and I'll get the poetry book for you."

Just then, the doorbell rang and Roxy opened the door. There stood a perplexed Eileen.

"If you're looking for Eric, he's in the bedroom," said Roxy with a smirk.

Eileen took one look at Roxy and threw the photos on the table saying, "Just give these photos to him, please." Then she turned and left.

Eric heard the door shut and rushed in to see Roxy holding the photos with a Cheshire cat smile on her face.

The implication couldn't be stronger.

Eileen quickly drove away, realizing that she was not a good judge of character and certainly not ready to enter the crazy dating world.

Eric was left standing in the doorway wondering what had just happened. He glared at Roxy, handed her the book, and she left quickly.

He sat at the table and placed one hand on the envelope of photos Eileen had thrown on the table. The other hand supported his bowed head. He felt defeated. How could he possibly explain the situation to her?

Nikki, Eileen's twenty-one-year-old daughter, had graduated from college in May and was looking forward to a summer vacation with her mother in Maine. Before leaving, she recognized she needed to break off her long-standing relationship with her boyfriend. For quite some time it had been obvious that the friendship was going nowhere. She had realized it wasn't enough for her simply to be comfortable with him. She felt no spark. And so, they had agreed to move on with no hard feelings. She left for the summer with a clear mind and a fresh start.

Once home, Eileen had to prepare for her daughter's arrival the next day. Nikki was a great kid! Eileen was so proud of her, and with reason. Nikki was vivacious, ambitious, and very smart. She looked like a younger version of her mother, but she wore her brown, curly hair down her back and had hazel eyes that flashed with intelligence. She had an athlete's figure due, in part, from years of soccer.

Mother and daughter were great friends and enjoyed hearing about each other's lives. They had a mutual respect for one another. Nikki was an artist like her mom and intended to use her talent in marketing, which had been her major in college. She hoped to go into advertising. Luckily, Nikki seemed to have an endless supply of creative ideas. Future singing lessons were also on her wish list.

Summer visits with Eileen were special to her, so Nikki decided to come sooner this time and surprise her mom. When she arrived a day early, Nikki found her mother with a troubled look on her face, sitting in the living room with a cup of tea.

"Mom, what's wrong?" she blurted out.

Nikki listened while fixing herself a pot of coffee. Since her dad had died, her mother hadn't shown any interest in another man.

There must be something very special about this man to have her become so emotionally involved, reasoned Nikki.

Eileen explained how Eric and she met and were hoping to see more of each other. She painted quite the colorful picture of Roxann. Nikki smiled, but listened intently to every word, not wanting to interrupt while her mom unburdened herself.

Now, it was Nikki's turn to talk. "Mom, I am sorry that this happened to you, but you are not thinking rationally. I don't know Eric, but there probably is a simple explanation that you never explored. As for Roxann—I have known girls like her at school who have everything handed to them and drive expensive cars. Some have even successfully traded sex for grades and find it an easy solution."

Eileen knew her daughter made sense. She hadn't given Eric a chance to explain anything when she bolted out of there. It was just too much to accept his innocence.

With a pained look on her face, she added, "I really don't want to see him, Nikki. How am I going to get those photos back?"

Nikki calmly sat down with her freshly-perked coffee and reassured her mom that things would be all right.

"Look, Mom, you don't have to face him; I will. I'll simply tell Eric you were busy and you sent me to pick up the photos."

Eileen decided that Nikki's idea made sense and offered a welcome relief from her problems.

"Okay, Nikki. I'm too drained to solve my own problems, so I'm turning them over to you. Besides, I need a second opinion on this whole scenario."

"There you go!"

Meanwhile, Eric fixed himself a stiff drink, which didn't help very much.

He thought back to when Eileen had first given him her business card and he had hurried home and looked up her website on his computer to check out her work and whatever else he could discover about this fascinating woman. When he read about a New York showing of her paintings, he also found an art critic's report:

Ms. Eileen Egan's paintings attracted a large crowd. Eileen flew in from her home in Maine to greet prospective buyers and admirers. Since the tragic car accident that took the life of her husband and partner, the well-known sculptor, Dan Egan, she closed their New York studio and moved to their cottage in Maine. She now has a studio in her home. This year's show lived up to expectations and, in some cases, surpassed the high standards art patrons had anticipated.

It went on to critique her works, but Eric had satisfied his curiosity about this intriguing woman.

He picked up the envelope and took out the photos. He saw their bench and pictured them sitting on it with his arm around her back. He shut his eyes to try and block out the image. It didn't help.

There were the little pink sneakers – Eileen's sneakers. He didn't know how long he stared at those photos while the memories they invoked flooded his troubled mind.

The next morning Eric went to the beach knowing full well what he would find – an empty bench with only sand around it. Although he was expecting to find her missing, it still caused an added ache to his heart. There he sat alone, listening to the angry surf smashing against the rocky shore. His emotions were stirred once again.

Since his wife's untimely death after only two years of marriage, he hadn't felt this deprived of such a precious part of his life. Marie had been everything to him and he had to watch it all end when cancer robbed him of his love. They were only in their mid-twenties and the last thing on their minds had been an end to their beautiful marriage. Yet, it did end, and with it the dreams of the family they had hoped to have. *Now, once again someone special to me has left and I can't do anything about it.* The roar of the ocean seemed louder and the mist in the air blended with the wet eyes he was trying to control. Perhaps if he looked hard enough, he would see Eileen walking in the distance. He knew that his mind could play tricks on him, so he shut his eyes and was lost in thought.

Eric had no idea how long he had sat there, but he knew she would not be coming. He went for his bike and slowly peddled home to his empty house.

Coffee was all he could stomach that morning.

And then the phone rang. "If that's Roxy, I'll slam it down before I say things that I will regret!"

After his chilly "Hello" he heard a pleasant voice say, "Hello, this is Eileen's daughter, Nikki. My mother is quite busy today, so I'll be coming over to pick up the photos so she'll know which one you have chosen for her to paint. If it's all right with you, I'd like to stop over now. Is this a good time?"

Eric was taken aback. He had never anticipated a call from her daughter. He wondered if there was hope after all. She didn't sound the least bit angry, so perhaps Eileen really does intend to go ahead with the painting, after all.

"Why, yes. Of course, I'd like to meet you. Did your mother give you directions?"

"Sure did. Be there in a couple of minutes."

Eric emptied the coffee pot and made a fresh pot for Nikki. He found himself pacing back and forth like someone had wound him up too tight. He just could not sit still with all this nervous energy inside him. Finally, he heard a car drive up and waited. He saw a lovely young woman get out and quickly walk to his door.

He opened the door to a smiling beauty with a strong resemblance to her mom. He saw no accusation in her eyes.

Eric smiled and asked her if she could stay for a quick cup of coffee. He told her how pleased he was that her mother agreed to do a painting for him and he pointed out where he hoped to hang it.

"Don't you agree that it will be a welcome addition to this place?"

"You know I am Mom's biggest fan, so, of course I agree."

"You must have heard about the uninvited guest that your mother met here yesterday?"

Before she had a chance to answer, Eric went on to explain about his troublesome student who claimed that she wished to do make-up work in order to graduate with her class.

Nikki listened as he mentioned that Miss Roxy Rehan would be staying at the most expensive place in the area, The Royal Haven Inn, and that he had his doubts about how much poetry Roxy would get around to reading. As he began to relax, Eric told her how much he enjoyed Eileen's company and hoped to continue seeing her. He even mentioned his past marriage and how he had never felt this taken with anyone since his Marie passed. After that, he handed over the photos and showed her his selection. As Nikki left, a relieved Eric waved her goodbye.

Nikki knew the inn where Roxy was staying. She'd spent many evenings visiting the piano bar, with their great pianist playing on a baby grand piano. The inn's restaurant had an outstanding reputation since they'd hired a well-known chef. Nikki felt another visit was in order.

The way she looked at it, Roxy would probably eat most of her main meals right at the inn. Nikki had been there once for a delicious meal. Roxy most likely would visit the bar first before leaving for the dining room. Nikki guessed she'd appear at five or five- thirty. With a little luck, she hoped she could spot her.

Nikki arrived at home just in time for lunch. Eileen had prepared one of Nikki's favorite lunches: crabmeat salad with a fresh green salad and French bread. Eileen looked up to see if she could read Nikki's conclusion by her facial expression. She was met with a big smile.

"I really like Eric, and he certainly seemed very sincere."

Then she went on to tell her about his student and why Roxy had been at Eric's cottage. Eileen felt foolish for having jumped to conclusions without first talking with Eric.

Nikki handed her the pictures and set aside Eric's choice. Eileen sighed when she saw that he had chosen the very one she had hoped he would select.

Nikki seemed deep in thought and then she looked up and said, "Mom, I'll be going out for a while. I'm not sure that I will be home for dinner, so don't plan anything special, okay?" Nikki liked to think that she left her mom feeling a little less upset than before her visit.

When Nikki arrived at the inn, there were people sitting on white rocking chairs and just relaxing on the long porch. When she opened the door, piano music wafted in, inviting her to come, listen, and forget any troubles.

John, the bartender and owner, spotted her as she entered the spacious room. He liked her looks and briefly wondered why she was all by herself. Waiting for someone, was his guess. She had on white slacks, white sandals and a silk blouse with bright flowers on a white background. Her brown hair was in a pony tail that bounced when she made her way to the bar and asked for lemonade with no ice. Nodding toward the pianist, she said to John, "He's really good, isn't he?" John liked it when customers appreciated a good pianist when they heard one.

"He sure is. He can play just about anything you can come up with and he even knows all the words. Now, how many guys can match that?" You could tell that John was a big fan.

"I think I'll grab that empty table near the piano and just enjoy listening." And she sat herself down and smiled at Ted, the pianist.

It was obvious to Ted that she was a music lover and that always made his job more pleasurable. Many evenings a group of young men who loved hearing songs from Broadway musicals gathered around the piano. Once he started playing for them, they would join in singing with such great voices that he felt they had probably been performers at some point in their lives. But this was a little early for that group.

Some businessmen deep in conversation with their briefcases near them found the inn's bar to be a great place to discuss their business in comfort. Some smiling couples were wrapped up in each other's conversations, and there were also five older women laughing over their drinks. Ted wondered if these ladies were all widows or if they just liked to go on vacation together. It was fun trying to guess what type of lives each one was leading. He looked again at Nikki and continued playing while he asked, "You're new here, aren't you?"

"Just checking out the place. I'm staying with my mother and wondered if she might like to come here some evening. I know that she'd just love your piano playing. Are you here most nights?"

"Not Monday and Tuesday. It's a great way to make a living—doing what I like to do and getting paid for it. You also get to meet some very interesting people and some regulars who end up becoming your friends."

Wanting to please her, he asked, "Anything I can play for you?"

"You might pick something from the *Phantom of the Opera*. I like the whole score."

That was a favorite with him, too. He immediately began playing "The Music of Your Life," and could hear her softly singing with a beautiful voice.

"Hey, you should come to the piano and sing it for us."

It was only then that Nikki realized he had been listening to her singing along.

"Honestly, no one will care. As you can see, they're all involved with each other." As she stood by the piano, Ted started playing it all over again from the beginning and Nikki sang out, watching him for any cues he might give her. The place went silent as everyone turned to listen to this new entertainment. When she had finished, they all clapped, much to Nikki's obvious surprise and embarrassment. Ted smiled and tried to encourage her to continue, but she sat down once again.

It was then that a young girl came in to view, who matched the vivid description Eileen had given Nikki of Roxy. She was really quite pretty, even with her rainbow-colored hair, Kelly green shorts, and a navy and matching green striped top, cut very low. Her sandals completed the outfit with green and navy straps. With head held high, she sauntered across the room, apparently very much aware of the stares. Once seated at the bar, she smiled at John.

"What will you have, young lady?"

"Gin and tonic will be fine."

Nikki watched her present an ID to the bartender and wondered if Roxy was underage. Using a fake ID would fit the personality of the young woman Eileen had described. However, if it were a fake, it must have been a good imitation, since the bartender accepted it and brought her the drink.

It appeared that the young woman intended to sit at the bar for a while before going to the dining room. Nikki waited until she had ordered a second drink before going to the bar to sit next to her.

Nikki ordered a Southern Comfort, looked at Roxy and said cheerfully, "I've been listening to the pianist. He's good, don't you think?"

Roxy seemed pleased to start a conversation and said, "Yeah, but I'd like to hear more stuff like country. You know what I mean?"

"You staying here?" inquired Roxy.

"No, but I like to stop in to hear the music and relax every once in a while. I need a break from the college grind. To spend the summer in Maine is my idea of heaven."

"You in college, too? I think they expect way too much from us, don't you?"

"I'll admit you have to work hard to get the grades that really count. Seems like I've spent too much time with my nose stuck in a book!"

"Boy, are you ever right about that! Like we don't have a life, ya know! I say you only live once, and you're only young once. Why waste those years studying when you could be out partying. Like, you know what I'm saying?"

Roxy's response led Nikki to feel that she'd established some common ground with her, and steered the conversation in another direction.

"That's true, but you can't do both, so you're more or less stuck studying. Right?"

"Well, not necessarily. It helps to know one of the teachers and maybe put a little pressure on him to raise your grade. Sometimes it works." She hesitated, as if she wasn't sure if she should go on, but she seemed eager to show Nikki how clever she was with her little act. Apparently her drinks had also lowered her reserves.

"As a matter of fact, one of my teachers lives up here and I found out about it. I tried first to see if I could take private lessons from him, if you know what I mean." She laughed and continued, "He wasn't having any of that, so I asked for a recommendation for a good book to self-study. Actually, he made a deal with me."

Uh, oh! What kind of a deal might that be? thought Nikki.

"He said that he had a poetry book in the bookcase in his bedroom, no less. He offered to loan it to me if I promised not to bother him the rest of the summer. He ended up giving me a big assignment" She laughed again. "But you ain't heard the best part yet! He told me to stay where I was and he started for the bedroom when this gal rang the doorbell. I answered it and she asked where Eric was. You should have seen the look on her face when I said he was in the bedroom! She tossed an envelope on the table and left." By now, Roxy was roaring with laughter.

Nikki thought, *Bingo!*

"So tell me how that's going to get you a higher grade? I must have missed something."

Roxy looked at her like she was stupid. "Well, now he just wants me out of the picture. I figure if I just do half my assignment, he'll accept that and forget about me."

"I guess I am just an old-fashioned girl because I like to earn my grades. Call it self-pride, if you will. You must really dislike this teacher."

"Naaah, as a matter of fact, all the students like him. He's a bit of a looker and knows his stuff." She frowned as the accusation sunk in, "Hey, what are you trying to do? Make me feel bad or something?"

"All in the way you look at it, I guess."

With that, Nikki smiled and left Roxy deep in thought.

Up in her room Roxy sensed that this whole scene was not turning out the way she thought it would. Somehow, her clever plot had taken a wrong turn. To her way of thinking, if the professor's friend arrived at the wrong conclusion, well, that's her fault. *This college girl thinks I should feel bad about that! No way!* And to stress her point, she kicked the dresser with all her might, leaving her with a very sore toe. Giving the whole scene a replay in her mind, Roxy thought maybe if she opened the book sitting in her room, she might figure out how to get a passing grade without resorting to deception.

When Roxy had been at the bar, she had assumed her conversation would remain private because the piano music would drown out her words. John, however, had learned to block out the music and hear conversations that were close to where he was standing. As he listened and watched Roxy's face, he thought he could see remorse in her expression. From his experience with the various clientele, he found that some people didn't realize how their actions looked until it was pointed out to them. He figured that, being young, she probably has never had anyone disagree with her in the past. His guess was that she wasn't really mean, just thoughtless.

Nikki realized that luck had been on her side. She had expected to spend at least two nights at the bar hoping to spot Roxy. Returning to the cottage, she entered the kitchen and was greeted by some tempting aromas. Eileen had prepared grilled salmon, macaroni and cheese casserole, and string beans. Nikki always looked forward to summer meals with her mom, even if she put on a couple of pounds in the process.

"Hey, Mom! I'm back early and I didn't eat out. You're making me hungry. Is it almost ready?"

"You timed it just right, Nikki. In ten minutes we can chow down together."

"Well, while we're waiting, why not sit down and listen to what I have to tell you." Nikki watched her mom's face as she detailed the exchange between Roxy and herself. When it was finished, Eileen got up and put her arms around her daughter.

"Wow! That was certainly enlightening. I can see that I arrived at all the wrong conclusions. Thanks, Nikki."

But when they sat down to dinner, it was hard for Eileen to enjoy her food when her mind was totally on Eric. Although Nikki seemed to have put the whole incident to rest with her description of her encounter with Roxy and was clearly savoring the meal, Eileen stopped eating. She felt certain Eric believed she had been left with the wrong impression, and she had to correct that as soon as possible. Eileen lost interest in dessert, and instead went to phone Eric.

Eric, in the meantime, couldn't concentrate on anything. He finally grabbed his bike and took off at top speed, wanting to get as far away as possible from where all this nonsense had taken place. With no idea where he was headed, he just wanted to keep moving. It really bothered him that this kind woman had such a mistaken opinion of him. When he finally realized that he was at the beach, he parked his bike and went to sit on the bench.

Back at his cottage, the phone rang without answer. Eileen had thought the moment had arrived to clear everything up between them. When that proved impossible, her determination increased. She took out her car keys and said, "I have to go looking for Eric. Have yourself another piece of pie and I'll be back as soon as I can."

Eileen thought Eric might be at the beach. Once there, she spotted his bike parked in the shade and she headed towards their bench. Eric turned and saw her just as she focused in on him. He stood up, an anxious look on his face. Eileen wore a big smile and waved before she got to him.

"Hi, Eric. You needn't look so concerned. I'm here to say that, yes, I did doubt you, but I no longer think that way. So, let's forget that whole unfortunate scene."

With visible relief, Eric said, "I don't know what happened to change your mind, Eileen, but I'm thankful we can put that behind us." Eileen snuggled up to him and he put his arm around her – two friends comfortable with each other, quietly listening to the sounds of the sea.

Time stood still for them as they watched the colors form in the evening sky and the sun begin to slowly sink in the distant horizon. As darkness covered the area, Eric looked at

Eileen and said, "I don't want this day to end, Eileen. Would you want to go somewhere for a drink?"

It didn't take Eileen very long to come up with an answer for, she too, wanted to extend their time together. "What about the inn Nikki went to today? She thought that the pianist was exceptionally good."

And so they ended up getting a small table near Ted's piano. He was just coming in from his break when he spotted the two of them. Something clicked when he looked at Eileen. Was it the smile or the way she held her head? And then it hit him. That young singer who had been here earlier bore a strong resemblance to this woman. He wondered if it was just a coincidence or if they were related.

Ted nodded in greeting to them and asked if there was anything special that they would like him to play. Eileen thought a minute and said, "Maybe something from *The Phantom of the Opera*?" Ted almost fell off his seat.

"You just have to be related to a young woman who was in here today! She answered the same way you just did."

Eileen giggled when she realized that she gave herself away. Nikki and she had the music from the show and played it often.

"Oh, you met my daughter, Nikki, didn't you?"

"Nikki. That name fits her. Did she tell you that we all got to hear her marvelous singing voice?"

"No, she didn't. Thank you for the compliment and I'd have to agree."

Ted went on to play while Eric and Eileen were completely focused on each other. Without realizing it, they were both leaning forward to shorten the distance between them. There was so much they wanted to know. Every detail of the other one's life seemed so important. Eric found her fascinating and couldn't believe his good fortune in finding her. Eileen respected his position in the college and admired his intelligence. They were so engrossed that they were unaware of the other tables slowly emptying all around them. Ted had stopped playing and he went to their table.

"Hey, you two. Do you know that you are the only ones left in here?"

They looked around in surprise at how swiftly the evening had passed. Reluctantly, they bid Ted goodbye and left hand in hand. With Eric's bike still in Eileen's car rack, she drove to his cottage,

"Will you be at the beach tomorrow or are you planning on sleeping late?"

"Sure, I'll be there for our walk. It's the best way to start my day!"

Chapter 4

Roxy had gone to her room after supper and put on boxer shorts and a tee shirt and kicked off her shoes. She noticed her toe was beginning to swell, so she put some ice in a face cloth as a temporary solution. Stashed away in her backpack, she had a bottle of her dad's wine. It wasn't all that strong but it would have to do. Plopped on her bed with her drink beside her, she opened the book with as much enthusiasm as she felt when opening the door to the dentist's office.

To her astonishment, Roxy really did understand what she was reading and found it intriguing. She had always liked hip-hop, and poetry had a similar beat. She began saying some of the poems out loud and anticipating the next rhyming word. It was more of a game than a lesson, and that was just fine with Roxy. When she discovered that she was moving on through the book, she felt a certain pride that comes with accomplishment.

When Eileen returned home and told Nikki about her encounter with Eric, Nikki was delighted that her mom and Eric had decided to go to the piano bar. She thought it was neat that Ted had seen the resemblance between the two of them. Because they were such great friends, she liked that they also looked alike. Besides, she thought her mom was beautiful, so Nikki had no complaints.

The next morning, Eric was waiting for Eileen, wearing a big grin on his face. Eileen couldn't help but smile, too. She took off her pink sneakers, making sure they were placed just where she had always put them, only this time his sandals were next to them in the sand.

Hand in hand, they headed towards the shore. The first icy waves hitting their feet made them pull back a little, but they soon accepted their initiation into a shore walk. The air seemed cleaner, the sun warmer, and the breeze more refreshing as they walked together. Everything he talked about somehow took on great importance to Eileen. Eric, in turn, gave her his total attention. They ended up walking a lot farther then they had intended and laughed about it. The way they felt at that time, they could have walked to the end of the beach without tiring.

They went to their bench to relax after their long walk and to extend their morning time together.

Eileen suggested that they have lunch at her place. Discovering that Eileen was an innovative cook was a surprise for Eric. He watched as she carefully selected from her large array of seasonings. Then she mixed sour cream, chopped olives, chives, and celery salt with tuna and spread it on wheat bread, followed by a few fresh leaves of lettuce. Some chips on the plates and ice tea in their glasses completed the lunch. Some people just have the knack of throwing ingredients together and having it work. Eileen was just such a person. Eric would have settled for crackers and peanut butter for lunch, so this was a real treat for him.

Roxy's cell phone played a silly tune and she answered with, "What's up?"

"Need me to liven up ya life, Babe?" Roxy heard the slow drawl of her sometime-boyfriend, Tex.

"Not really. It's not bad up here. Real ritzy place. What have you been up to while I've been gone?"

"Been doin' a lot of traveling. With the gas prices so high, it's tough to make it as a truck driver. Been thinkin' about getting a job 'round here – more steady and less worries. How's that Mercedes of yours doin'?"

"Nice to know how much ya miss me, Tex. All you really miss is drivin' my car."

"Hey, Babe. That ain't all I miss, if you know what I mean!" he chuckled.

"Yeah, yeah! Tell me another."

Having been away from Tex and his crazy crowd, Roxy saw him in a new light. She realized now that he never made her feel important in his life. He was good for laughs and some excitement whenever she felt bored. He earned the name, Tex, because he loved country music and wore his cowboy hat for most of his waking hours. Roxy was certainly aware of other girls in his life, although she was his favorite. She knew Tex liked the idea that money wasn't important to Roxy, so she could afford to pay for their evening's entertainment. Although hating to admit it, she was a cheap date. Right now, she didn't miss the guy.

"So, I was thinkin' some time I might take a ride up there and remind you what you've been missin'." Roxy didn't find that amusing. He could be such a conceited jerk at times.

"Naw. I don't think so. This is not the type of place that would excite you, Tex. Much too proper for you, and I wouldn't want you to feel out of place. Okay?" It was more of a statement then a question. The last thing she felt like was putting up with his crazy antics and getting her kicked out of here.

"Yeah, I guess you're right! I'll probably wait 'til you're so damn bored that you beg me to come up there. And who knows, if you're lucky I just might say yes." With that declaration, he hung up.

As the days passed, Roxy spent more and more time at the lounge in her seat by the piano. She had her book with her each time, and the piano music somehow helped her with the poetry she was reading. She found that she could relax and find enjoyment in this poetry stuff. That was a pleasant surprise to her.

Ted watched with amusement at the incongruous sight of this bohemian girl intently reading poetry. Once in a while, she would look at him like she was trying to digest what she was reading. He liked what he saw in that complicated face. Ted felt he could read so many people by looking at their faces, but not this girl. He knew she was still trying to find herself and perhaps wondering what direction she might take. Beyond that, he had no idea what she was like, but he sure would like to know if she would be receptive to any advances on his part.

"How are you coming along with your poetry book?"

She had been so intent on her studies that his question startled her. "Oh, yeah! I kind of like this stuff! You know much about it?"

"No, I know nothing about it. Any free time that I have, I like to dabble in making up songs. I guess I'm just a frustrated, would-be songwriter at heart."

Roxy gave him a big smile that encouraged him to continue.

"I see you here so often I'd like to put a name to such a pretty face."

Roxy liked that approach: polite, but to the point.

"Roxann Rehan, but you can call me Roxy. And your name is?"

"Ted Logan. Anything in particular that you would like to have me play for you?"

"Well, you said that you have some of your own compositions. Do you have anything kind of quirky?"

Ted laughed. It fit what he thought she might request.

"Let's see. How about this silly little ditty?" And he played a perky, catchy song – the kind that would stick in your head long after you'd heard it. Roxy seemed to love it. All the while he played, she used her forefingers to tap out the rhythm. Since there were so few in the bar at this early hour, she asked him to play it again. Ted was beaming. That she really liked something he wrote, he found amazing!

Roxy was listening with a concentrated expression. All the poetry she'd been exposed to in the past week was stuck in her head and began to form lively lyrics to accompany the music he played. She had a pad with her for taking down notes as she studied. Now she used it to jot down what was coming to her fast and furious. Ted watched her out of the corner of his eye and thought she'd lost interest in his song, so he cut it short.

"What did you stop for?" she yelled at him. "Can't you see I'm trying to write the words for your song?"

Ted was astonished! It was the last thing he could have imagined! He went back to playing it again from the beginning, all the while hoping no one at the bar would wonder what the heck he was doing.

Roxy reread what she had written and then handed it to Ted. "See how you think this fits!" she asked. He stopped playing to read the new lyrics and laughed out loud.

"Hey, these lyrics fit just fine, Roxy. Not at all what I would have come up with, but your choice of words is better. What a clever girl you are!"

Roxy beamed. She had never attempted anything like that before and didn't know why she did it now. To receive such an unexpected compliment from someone like Ted was a treasure for Roxy.

Ted tried singing the words even though he didn't feel his voice was anything exceptional. It was then that he noticed John, the bartender, looking their way and giving Ted a thumbs-up. Ted kept going until he sang the last note. To his surprise, the few patrons in the bar were clapping and smiling. Later John caught up with Ted and said he really liked the song and asked him to give it a try that night.

Roxy and Ted were both laughing now and he decided to take his piano break while she was in such a good mood. Without bothering to ask her permission, he sat at her table and asked where she learned to write like that.

Roxy had never thought about writing, so she had no answer for him.

"So, Ted. Tell me about yourself. How old are you and are you hitched?"

Ted expected this kind of bluntness from her and it amused him that he was right. He let her know that he was twenty-two and had never been married. He had majored in music in college and had played wherever he could to earn money while at school. Now that he had graduated, he was grateful to be playing full-time at the inn. He had dated, but nothing serious.

Being only twenty, she was not sure where she wanted to go or what she wanted to do. She revealed that she didn't have a serious boyfriend in her life, so Ted racked up the courage to ask her out to dinner.

It thrilled Roxy and she readily accepted. They agreed to go next door to the dining room at his dinner break.

Feeling confident, Roxy picked up her pad and book and headed toward her room. Checking her wardrobe to see if she had packed anything that would look proper and stylish for the occasion, she chose a white linen skirt that fell just above her knees. A black and white checked silk blouse with cape sleeves went well. Next, she found a thick, black leather belt, a small black purse and black leather sandals. That was the best she could come up with, so it would have to do.

Now for a check of her makeup: she looked closely at her heavily made-up face. Somehow it didn't seem like the look that Ted would like. She ended up doing something that Roxy had never done before—removing all her make-up and leaving her face scrubbed free and glowing. She liked her bright red lipstick so that stayed, but she used a smaller amount of mascara on her eyelashes. Yet her rainbow hair color remained a puzzle. Again she looked through her collection of clothes for an idea. There was a white silk scarf and she studied it for a few seconds. She pulled her hair up and then twisted the scarf around her head, covering the hair except for the very top of the crown, as she still liked showing her unique hair coloring. Searching through her jewelry, she located a pretty diamond broach and fastened it onto the scarf.

One last glance in the mirror, and she proc
too bad! As long as Ted thinks so, that's all I care."

Ted went to his usual table and let the waitress know he
was expecting a guest. He ordered a good wine and anxiously
watched the doorway. And what an entrance she made! Roxy
was a knockout! This time when heads turned her way, it was
in complete admiration for a very attractive young woman.
She stopped and glanced around the room and lit up when
she spotted the handsome young man at the corner table. Ted
liked her lively step as she came over to him.

"I ordered us some wine, forgetting that you're under
twenty-one. I really don't think anyone will question us if
you'd like to try a glass." Ted said, embarrassed by his
mistake.

Roxy laughed, "Hey, if I had a nickel for every glass of
wine I've tasted, I would be rich. Besides, tonight I think I
look older than I am, right?"

Ted agreed and poured out the wine for them. "To new
friends and a new song," he said as they touched glasses in a
toast.

Although the meal was excellent, neither one of them
paid all that much attention to it. They were far too busy
making plans for his days off. For starters, there was a
comedy playing at the local playhouse which neither one had
seen. There were also some good movies. Even just seeing a
movie took on a greater interest for her.

Ted had to go back to work after dinner, but Roxy didn't
mind joining him in the lounge and sitting there listening to
him playing. She admired his talent and marveled at the way

...usic sheet in front of him. Now, that

...ouple could be found in Eric and Eileen, ...us few weeks of shared time. They went ...rides, stopping at small antique stores and scenic... As for the painting assignment, Eileen set aside four hours each day to work in her studio, which was far less time then she usually planned to paint. She found herself humming a lot, too.

They decided to go to the lounge one Saturday night. When they entered and looked for an empty table by the piano, they spotted Roxy. She looked like a very different Roxy than either of them remembered. This girl was watching the pianist with rapt attention. They started to back out of the room when Roxy caught sight of them.

Their eyes met and Roxy jumped up and rushed to them. She looked delighted to see them and they were understandably puzzled.

"Professor Ames, have I got news for you!" she couldn't wait to tell him. "I understand poetry." She caught his skeptical expression. "No, seriously, I do. I've been putting in a lot of hours reading that book of yours." She pointed to Ted. "You can ask the pianist 'cause that's where I do my studying."

"Well, you'll have to admit, Roxy, it's hard to believe you would do that on your own."

"Ain't it the truth? But I'm three quarters through the book, and that is with rereading the pages until I really get it. Know somethin' else?" Eric shook his head in answer. "I found out that I like it. Seriously, I like playing with words. In fact, I may just take your grammar class this coming semester."

She had a determined look on her face that led them to believe that she was sincere.

Eric could hardly believe his ears! What happened to that other Roxy? What caused the big change? All three walked over to a table near Ted. Eric ordered drinks for them.

Roxy looked at Eileen with some concern. She seemed to want to say something, but just went back to her drink.

Eileen found herself actually rooting for her. She was certain Roxy would be quite the challenge for Eric, but she knew he was up to it.

Then all three focused on the girl coming in to the bar. It was Nikki. Seeing Roxy sitting with them was a surprise.

Roxy let out a yell and said, "Hey, that's the girl I met before."

Nikki didn't know quite what to do. She came to their table and said, "Hi all."

Now it was Roxy who was confused. She couldn't figure out the connection. Nikki pulled up a chair and sat down with them. It was then that Eric explained everything to Roxy.

She didn't like being tricked but, on second thought, she realized the girl was clever. They exchanged names and soon Roxy was excitedly telling them about Ted and his new song. Looking at Eric, she told him how she had written the words to it.

Ted had been listening to the conversation and put two and two together. Now, it all made sense. He remembered seeing the two girls at the bar and wondering what the conversation was all about. Knowing Nikki liked music, he asked if she wanted to hear the song that Roxy was talking about, and of course, she did.

Ted played it, much to the delight of Roxy. He still had the paper with Roxy's lyrics on it and he handed it to Nikki. The broken English fit the catchy tune and Ted played it again so that Nikki could see how well it matched up. Then Ted asked Nikki to sing it, hoping that she would do justice to the song. They all encouraged Nikki and it was a fun song, so she stood at the piano and sang it.

"Hot damn," exclaimed Roxy "That song is perfect for her. Isn't this exciting?"

Laughing, they looked up to see John coming to their table and thought maybe they were a bit too loud, but instead, John congratulated Nikki on her rendition of the song.

"I don't suppose that you would consider working here one night a week? It really adds to the entertainment to have a vocalist here. You could name your night if you like, but I was really hoping you could come on Saturday night. What do you think?"

Nikki was taken aback. That was the last thing she had expected to be asked.

"Gee, thanks for the compliment, but I'm not a professional singer."

"That's not a problem. Would you just think about it? Okay?"

Her fans at the table all thought it a great idea. It was only for one night and why not?

"Well, if you think it would work out. I'd have to study with Ted to see if I know the words to the songs he'd be playing. If I did this, it certainly wouldn't be on a Saturday night until I knew how well we progressed."

Ted was pleased at this new turnabout. He thought Nikki would be fun to work with, so it was certainly all right with him.

He wanted to encourage her and said, "Let's give it a try, Nikki."

The following morning Nikki met with Ted and, uninvited, Roxy showed up, too. Roxy hated to admit that she was feeling a little possessive towards Ted and wanted to make certain that the spark in his eye was only for her. For the next three mornings, the three of them got together for rehearsing and it was working out better than they had hoped for.

Nikki's love of music paid off, because she had no trouble remembering the lyrics of the songs Ted chose to play. A side benefit to all this was a close friendship that was developing between the two girls. Nikki found Roxy to be a colorful character with a big heart. Roxy held Nikki in high esteem and secretly aspired to be more like her.

After the third morning, Ted suggested a tryout with the afternoon clientele. This was all so new to Nikki, but she felt comfortable with Ted accompanying her on the piano, so she agreed to give it a try. Roxy had become a permanent fixture there and she watched these two talented people with a deep appreciation that also encouraged Ted and Nikki to earn that praise.

As a few patrons entered the bar, Ted signaled Nikki and the music started. Most of the regulars to the lounge were accustomed to the piano playing and they were pleasantly surprised as Nikki began to sing. Her strong voice carried out into the nearby dining room and people began to listen. Ted knew what songs complimented her voice the best, most of which turned out to be Broadway musical compositions. Nikki lost her inhibition and gave it her all. More and more people drifted in out of curiosity. When she finished her song, she was startled by the loud round of applause. Both Ted and John knew they were onto something. This girl could easily become a star if she had exposure.

Roxy acted as if Nikki was her discovery and beamed at the response to her song. With all this encouragement, Nikki moved about holding the mike and stopping at different tables. Ted was really proud of his find and looked over at John, who gave him the okay sign. The more responsive the patrons, the more Nikki seemed to give back, and she could really belt out a song with little effort.

The bar welcomed the largest afternoon crowd they had seen all summer. This caused John to ask Nikki if she might reconsider that Saturday night offer. He also thought that adding a second night would be a good drawing card if this was a sample of what they could expect to hear.

Nikki experienced a natural high from all the accolades, but everything was happening too fast. Yes, she might try the Saturday night gig, but adding more nights would have to wait awhile.

After Nikki's performance, the three of them lingered in the bar, obviously pleased with the entertainment.

"All this makes me feel as good as smoking a joint," Roxy loudly proclaimed. They laughed with her in agreement. Nikki asked for one more rehearsal before attempting to sing before the Saturday night crowd. They thought that was a good idea, and agreed to meet the next day.

Chapter 5

The next morning, Nikki, John, and Roxy met in the lounge and went over the list of songs that Ted had drawn up for consideration. Nikki liked his taste and only rejected one on the list.

They enjoyed working in the well-lit lounge. A wall of windows looked out onto a patio and parking area. When the loud sound of a revving motorcycle interrupted their conversation, they all looked up at the window. Roxy was hoping she wouldn't see who she suspected might be out there. She rushed over to the window and there was Tex, as big as life, taking off his helmet. Trying to head him off, she went to the entrance and met him as he was coming inside.

"Tex, what are you doing here?" It was obvious that she was upset by his arrival.

"Hey, Babe. Where's the open arms greeting I was expecting?"

"I have plans for my time here and, keep in mind, that I didn't invite you, Tex."

"And what could be more important than being with your Tex?"

"You're not MY Tex."

"What the hell is this? You're breaking up with me?"

"Tex," Roxy said exasperated, "you go out with any babe you feel like, but you expect me to be with just you? Is that right?"

"Yeah, that's right! I thought that you were honored that I picked you the most!"

"Well, I'm not!"

Roxy was at a loss as to how to get him out of the place. She could see he was headed right for the lounge.

"First-class place you got here! Guess it makes ya think that you're pretty high class, too. Right, Rox?"

Meanwhile, Nikki, John, and Ted were wondering just what was going on. They could see that these two knew each other, but Roxy didn't look happy to see him. Tex was a big guy with piercings that held gold rings in his ears, eyebrows and nostrils. His exposed arms were covered with tattoos of girls in various poses. His hair was long and in a ponytail, and sideburns made their way down his cheeks to form a scraggly beard. He had on a black leather vest and jeans with holes in them. Not exactly the type of customer John wanted at his bar.

"Hit me with a cold beer!" he said to John.

Roxy stood beside him with a pained look on her face.

"John, this is Tex. He lives near my school and he decided to ride his bike up here to check out the area."

Tex lost his cool and raised his voice.

"Oh, it's John, is it? On a first-name basis. You been messin' around, Rox?"

"Screw you, Tex! I want you out of here. I'm here to study and you're the one who's messing things up."

"Why you little tramp! You dare talk to me like that?" He grabbed her arm and squeezed it hard enough to make her wince. Ted and Nikki ran over to Roxy. John came out from behind the bar to join them.

"Take your hands off of her! Now!" shouted Ted. John got on one side of Tex and Ted got on the other. They made it clear that they were leading him outside.

The hate that showed on his face scared Roxy. "I won't forget this, Roxy. When you're aching for excitement in your life, don't call on me 'cuz you're through being my bitch." After literally being pushed out the door, Tex got on his bike and revved it as loud as he could and then sped off.

Roxy was visibly shaken from the conflict. She knew that Tex changed when he didn't get his way, but this display of temper frightened her.

Ted was back and came to her with great concern. He held her in his arms and noticed that she was shaking. Her tough appearance was so deceptive, yet he wanted to protect her from ever getting threatened again.

"You okay, hon?"

The stark difference between the two men in her life was apparent to all of them. Roxy considered herself lucky to have found this decent man and vowed she would do her best to hang onto him.

John pulled a chair out for her and brought her a glass of water. It might have been champagne for the appreciation she felt toward him. Their sincere concern for her left a lasting impression with Roxy.

Once Roxy got her composure back, Ted and Nikki continued with their rehearsal. All agreed that she was ready for her Saturday night performance.

When Saturday night arrived, the lounge was filled to capacity. Word had spread that there was a new singer at the inn. It was good that Nikki didn't know that, because she didn't need any added pressure to do well. John decided that he'd be the one to introduce her, because he was so proud of her.

Dressed in a soft lavender frock with teal blue trimming gathered with a lavender and teal belt emphasizing the smallness of her waist, she looked like a model. Her mom had painted her sandals with the two colors for coordination. Her hair was done up for added height and confidence. Topped with light makeup, her tasteful outfit was complete. Just looking at her seemed to delight the crowd.

John beamed, "Well, folks, you're in for a treat tonight. Most of you know Ted Logan, our talented pianist." John nodded toward him. "Now, I want you to listen to the beautiful voice of Nikki Egan. Let's give her a hand." John led and they followed with a polite clapping. Ted played an introductory bit of the well-known Broadway song, "New York, New York," and Nikki started to sing. No one spoke and waitresses stopped in their tracks as Nikki's powerful voice filled the room. You could see feet and hands tapping out the rhythm as if joining in and helping her along. When she reached the last note, Nikki held it and threw her arms in the air bringing down the house. They whistled and cheered and stood and clapped. Nikki watched in disbelief at this reaction. She tried to hold back the tears of appreciation for this reception, but her eyes filled to the brim. Ted, too, was so happy for her that his eyes were misty. In the doorway stood Eileen and Eric, who had come too late for a seat but not too late to hear her first song. They wouldn't have missed this for the world!

The whole evening was a tribute to Nikki. The customers treated her as if she were a Broadway star. Instead of talking to each other and accepting the entertainment as background music, they listened to each song she sang. John was convinced that hiring her was an amazing business feat on his part. He stuck out his chest while waiting on the clientele.

Then Ted rose, grabbed her hand and the two of them bowed for the newfound fans. Eric and Eileen came over to their table and joined Roxy, Nikki, and Ted. When the lounge was empty, John came over, too. John said he had been thinking that maybe he would take reservations on Saturday nights. In fact, he might have two shows. People could make reservations for either the early performance or the later one.

Ted laughed and looked at his friend. "John, you have dollar signs in your eyes."

John had to admit, Ted was right. He could advertise and even use Nikki's marketing skills to promote his new strategy. Of course, he'd pay her well since he would, indeed, be earning more money. When he closed the bar and everyone went home, his mind was going full steam and things were looking up.

Eileen kissed Eric goodnight and went home with Nikki. It was late and they were all emotionally drained. What a great night it had been!

Over the next week, Nikki was busy designing advertising pieces to submit to the local newspaper and making up posters to place in stores. John had insisted that she use a professional photographer to take her picture singing close to Ted as he played the piano. At Eileen's urging, she bought a rose-colored dress that showed off her lovely figure. The ads mentioned the two performances and suggested phoning early for reserved seating. Nikki thought that John was going overboard with all this fuss, but she was using her talents and enjoying her job.

Eric found himself thinking of Roxy and her new attitude and sensed he could help her if she were sincere, but he wondered if this was a passing phase or if she was up to something. He felt that, as her teacher, he should give her the benefit of the doubt and offer her a few private lessons. He had to admit, he was wary of having her at his house alone with him. Finally, he came up with the only solution he could think of, which was to ask Eileen if he could teach Roxy in her kitchen while she painted in the next room. Eileen agreed, and when he presented his plan to Roxy, she was thrilled to be given a second chance. Twice a week, she arrived at the appointed time and surprised herself, as well as Eric, when she proved to be such a dedicated student.

As Roxy's grasp of English improved, she started writing poetry with the intention of helping Ted with his lyrics. It was all the incentive that she needed and, when ready, she asked Ted to play her the other songs he had written. They ended up spending hours on his days off composing many beautiful songs.

Roxy was optimistic and relied on her father to figure out a way to have the songs recorded. She didn't want a guarantee, just a hearing. If they could get their foot in the door, just maybe, they stood a chance. As for Ted, he thought she was a wonderful dreamer, but that was all right because he enjoyed every minute working with her. Ted knew that she tried so hard just to please and that she believed in his talent. That thrilled him!

After three weeks of promoting the Saturday night performances, the results were more than John had hoped for. They now had sold-out bookings. With this success, Nikki asked Ted and Roxy if she could sing a few of their songs and get some audience feedback on them. They all agreed that this was a good test to see if the songs really were worth pushing further.

Monday morning found Nikki, once again, rehearsing with Ted, determined to polish their act to their satisfaction.

The following Saturday night, John took the mike and announced that the audience was about to hear three songs composed by Ted and Roxy and sung by Nikki – a collaboration of these three talented people right here. Everyone was quiet as Ted began to play the introduction to a very romantic number. Nikki sang the words with so much feeling that it touched the emotions of everyone in the room. She knew when to sing softly and when to belt it out and it was this coloring that brought the songs to life for the listeners. At the end of the performance, they received a standing ovation, giving all the encouragement Ted and Roxy needed to continue composing. They did, indeed, make a great team.

When closing time came, one middle-aged gentleman remained behind. Walking over to Ted he asked to speak with him about his songs. Roxy and Nikki joined them at their table.

"I work as a disc jockey at a Boston radio station. With my job I hear all kinds of music and as a result I am a good judge of what is good and what is not. I want to tell you people that I am very impressed with the songs you played tonight. Now, if you could come up with some additional songs of the same caliber and have a demo recording made professionally, I am sure that I could arrange to have it played. Is this something that you would be interested in doing?"

They looked a little dumbfounded at hearing this proposition but managed to tell him that it sounded good to them, and they would give it a lot of thought. The man left his business card and told them to get in touch when they had completed a recording. With that, he left and all three let this suggestion sink in.

Roxy spoke first, "Ted, how many other songs have you composed so far?" When Ted said about seven more, Roxy was all fired up. "Wow, have we got our work cut out for us! We'll aim for completing one a week and Eric can check out my lyrics for grammatical errors. In addition to your days off, we can work mornings. How's that grab ya. Oops! I mean, 'How does that sound to you?'"

Ted had a concerned look on his face. "Look, let's not have anything written in stone just yet, okay? This is a huge undertaking and I am not sure that any of us is really up to it."

"Don't put a damper on this, Ted! This guy wouldn't have approached us if he didn't think that we stood a chance. We'll start with just one new song Monday morning and see if all three of us agree that it's a future hit like the other ones." When Ted just looked at her, she said, "Damn, Ted. Just go for it!"

Inspired by Roxy's passion, Ted worked with her every day during the next week. Eric checked the results and offered suggestions whenever Roxy presented the lyrics to him. It was also a good time to give her a few grammatical rules to keep in mind as she pushed her brain to make up for lost time, as she put it. By the end of the week, they had met their deadline after much rewriting. But these revisions turned out a polished version of the new song and when Nikki finally heard it, she agreed that it was another winner.

Roxy was a quick learner and her exposure to the extensive vocabulary of Eric and her new friends soon erased the old habits. "Ain't" had disappeared altogether and she found it amusing that the double negatives she was used to hearing really meant just the opposite. With her renewed enthusiasm for learning, Roxy tackled one song after another and found it easier with each new song. Ted agreed that she had a talent for poetry. She knew he was her biggest fan and the easiest to please. Eric would critique with his red pencil, but that is what she expected and wanted.

Roxy decided it was time to phone home and surprise her parents with the progress she'd made in her education through her own hard work. Anne Rehan wasn't all that happy when she heard her daughter's voice. The first thing that crossed her mind was, *What does she want now?* Roxy blurted out a summary of all that had gone on while she was away. Anne could hardly believe her ears! It wasn't just the excitement in her voice, but it was this new way of talking that amazed Anne. The last thing she expected was that her daughter was interested in poetry! And now she was writing the lyrics to songs! Anne couldn't wait to tell Jack of the miraculous change that had taken place in such a short time.

Jack must have talked the professor into giving Roxy private lessons after all.

"Mom, you and Dad have got to come up here for the Saturday night concert. I can reserve you a table right up front and I can guarantee that you will just love it! What do you say?"

When Anne finally got her bearings, she replied, "Well, sure, I don't see why not, if you're that enthusiastic about it! Now, I did get this straight, didn't I? You wrote the lyrics to songs that we will be hearing? This is no joke, Roxy, is it?"

"Thanks for the vote of confidence, Mom!"

Tears were in Anne's eyes now as she began to digest what Roxy had said. This was more than she had ever hoped would happen, and wild horses wouldn't keep her from being there on Saturday. *Jack will be shocked when I tell him*, she thought as she hung up the phone.

When Jack finally came home, Anne's elation hadn't petered out one iota. She rushed to greet him with so much news that she hardly took a breath. Jack's reaction was one of skepticism. This definitely didn't sound like his Roxy. However, Anne's enthusiasm was contagious and he agreed to join her in visiting their daughter. He didn't wait a minute to phone the inn to make certain they had reservations for overnight and for the concert. When he said that he was Roxy's dad, they assured him he'd have one of their best rooms and a special table in the lounge. Now, that was a new experience for Jack, as it seemed Roxy was the one pulling the weight this time.

As their BMW pulled up to the inn, they spotted Roxy sitting on the front porch waiting for their arrival. She had a notebook in her lap and had been writing until she heard their car pull up. What a pleasant surprise to see the happy expression on Roxy's face as she hurried to meet them! And, just as surprising, were the tasteful outfit she wore and the normal hair coloring. Missing, also, was the heavy makeup. She greeted each one with a kiss that left them beaming.

Roxy carried the luggage for Anne and brought them to the desk clerk. She introduced her parents, which produced a cheerful response. They were given a lovely room with a view of the ocean. Sliding doors opened onto a small balcony with comfortable, white wicker chairs and a table. Roxy helped them unpack, all the while chatting away about her new life up here. She spoke of her friends, including the professor, with real affection. Anne kept glancing over at Jack to see if he was as overcome as she was by the strange metamorphosis they were witnessing.

"Do you need to rest first, or can we go downstairs for a drink?" Roxy asked excitedly. "That is where my new friends are and I can't wait to have you meet them. They're awesome!"

"Let me just freshen up a bit, hon, and then we'll go downstairs. Why don't you go down and we'll meet you there in just a few minutes?"

Roxy left the two of them looking at each other in disbelief! Both of them had been expecting her to revert back to the old Roxy.

"This just seems too good to be true, Jack! I don't know about you, but I am thrilled over the change."

"Let's not question it. Let's just enjoy it while it lasts. I'm anxious to meet these friends who were instrumental in this turn-about. They did what all my money never accomplished and I want to shake their hands. As soon as you're ready, we'll head downstairs, Anne."

Once downstairs, they went straight for the lounge, where they found Roxy anxiously awaiting their arrival. She ran to them, took each of their hands and led them over to Ted, who rose up to greet them.

Jack immediately liked him, especially his firm handshake. Anne was impressed with the way he looked her in the eyes as they were introduced.

"I suppose that Roxy has told you all about our plans!" Ted asked.

Roxy didn't wait for their answer and popped up with, "Well, of course, I did! What a silly question! I want them to know all about you, Ted, before you go on stage."

They sat there for an hour getting to know this polite, talented young man. Roxy kept egging him on with "Tell them about—," and "Tell them about—." She wanted them to know just about everything there was to know about this wonderful guy. And then she told them the most important news, that they were a couple. Her parents couldn't have been more pleased about that.

When Ted left the table to play a few songs before Nikki arrived, Roxy immediately asked her parents, "Sooooo? What did you think?"

"I think I can speak for your mother, as well as myself, in saying we like him very much."

"Oh, Dad. He's the greatest!"

When Nikki entered the lounge, she came over to them. Roxy introduced her and they talked awhile. The place was beginning to fill up for the first show. Jack and Anne looked at this lovely young lady in her cream-colored, lace gown and they understood why Roxy admired her friend so much.

Eric and Eileen wandered in just minutes before the start of the show, knowing they had a table waiting for them. They were pleased to meet Roxy's parents and anxious to see their initial reaction when they heard the songs. Ted signaled for Nikki to start and the place went quiet.

Anne and Jack were pleasantly surprised! Not only was the music appealing, but their daughter's lyrics warmed their hearts. That Roxy had possessed this talent was a shock to both of them. Who knew?

At intermission, Jack thanked Eric for the change in his Roxy. He wanted to make out a big check for him, but Eric refused.

"My payment was seeing her transformation. I didn't think that she could do it, but I was proven wrong. Had you told me that she was capable of writing song lyrics, I would have said you were crazy! Roxy is the rare case that every teacher hopes will come his or her way. I'm just glad that it happened to me. It also makes me wonder if she has other talents for us to discover. I know that once Roxy has made up her mind to do something, she follows through until reaching her goal. That's a powerful trait and it should take her far."

After the lounge closed, Roxy and her parents lingered in the lobby, still basking in the warmth of the evening.

Chapter 6

As much as Eileen enjoyed being with Eric, she felt it necessary to limit their togetherness. So most weekdays, after their morning walks, they went their separate ways. Eric reluctantly accepted this arrangement.

Eileen decided to surprise Eric when Nikki left for rehearsal. She phoned Eric to let him know that she'd be walking to the grocery store for some fresh food, but hoped to be back by five. Once home, they could plan on preparing and sharing supper.

It was a short walk and welcome exercise. She limited her selections to spaghetti sauce, grated cheese and bread sticks, just enough to fill her paper bag. As she headed home the sky suddenly darkened and the rain began to fall. Eileen quickened her steps.

Eric, in the meantime, saw the storm approaching and immediately grabbed his umbrella and rushed to his car. He hoped to find her before she left the store. By the time he saw her, she was almost home and still running.

Eric parked the car and hurried with his umbrella just as she started up the driveway. By now, the umbrella was useless, as Eileen was soaked to the skin. It was at this point that the paper bag gave way, spilling all the food at her feet.

They both looked down at the puddles of red sauce mixed with grated cheese, soggy bread sticks and broken glass. Eileen gazed up through wet strands of hair and saw the bewildered expression on Eric's face, and laughing, she said, "Well, that worked out well, didn't it?"

They left the mess and ran in the house dripping a trail behind them. Before Eileen went to change, Eric stopped her. "Don't move!" He took out his cell phone and took a picture of her. "This is a photo I will always treasure, Eileen. Thank you for this moment." Then he kissed her before letting her go to change into dry clothes.

While she changed, Eric decided to start supper for her. He found a large pot and filled it with water and turned on the stove. Checking the cupboard, he located a box of pasta. By the time she returned, it was cooked. He asked if she had any stewed tomatoes and cheese, which she did. While he finished putting the pasta together, Eileen made a lettuce, tomato, and cucumber salad. All and all, they were able to come up with a passable meal.

"I don't think that we should open a restaurant, Eileen. But we do make a good team."

A disc was playing soft background music they had selected from her vast collection. Eric stood up and, without saying a word, opened his arms to her and they fell into step to the romantic music playing.

The closeness stirred their emotions and Eric tenderly kissed her. Her passionate response was more than he had bargained for and he no longer could hold back his desire. All Eileen's reserve disappeared and they locked in an embrace. Their breathing increased as he pushed her tightly against his ready body. Eileen tipped her head back with a sigh, causing Eric to whisper, "Eileen, I don't want to stop now."

"Neither do I," was all he needed to hear and he swept her up in his arms and carried her to the bedroom, where all the hidden passion that they both felt for each other spilled forth in a heated fury. As Eileen wrapped her body around his muscular frame, they became one. Eric couldn't get enough of her and Eileen didn't want it to end. The strength of the electric feelings was heightened by the tender words they expressed to one another.

When their lovemaking ended, they remained in an embrace, savoring the precious moment. They let the feeling of total contentment flow over them and neither questioned in their minds the feelings they now shared.

Much later, Eileen walked him to his car and they stopped to admire the clear night sky. Eric pointed out some of the constellations that were visible in the summertime.

"I find it fascinating to realize that these same stars have taken on such great meaning to people down through the ages—even to the point of letting the stars guide and direct their future lives. I like to picture the sailors of long ago, depending on the night sky as their first GPS. It was certainly of dire importance at that time. And too, I wonder who decided that a particular group of stars seemed to form a recognizable picture? Lots to ponder when gazing at a night sky."

Eileen had her head tipped back to look up and Eric bent down and kissed her goodnight. She still felt the effects of his kiss as she watched him drive away, looking forward to more togetherness to come.

The next morning, after their beach walk, they decided to eat breakfast at the inn, hoping to catch sight of Roxy's parents once more. They were just starting to eat when her parents came in and joined them. It was a chance to get to know this nice couple a little better. Just as they expected, Jack proved to be an interesting and knowledgeable man.

Jack said he had been in real estate for years and he talked about the big changes he has seen lately. The big estates that he had dealt with weren't moving nearly as fast as they had in the past. He had to advise his clients to lower their asking price, and that didn't settle very well. Jack used to enjoy his business and the social part of meeting so many interesting people. "It's a changing world," he said. Now, he wanted to know what made Eric tick.

"Say, Eric, Roxy has mentioned that you are writing a novel. Is that so?"

"Just a summer pastime, Jack."

Like his daughter, Jack didn't beat around the bush when he had something to say. "Would you consider it too presumptuous of me if I asked you to allow me to read it?"

Eric seemed embarrassed by this stranger's request. "Well, no, but why would you want to read it?"

"I just think that an English professor might also be a good writer. If you feel this is an invasion of your privacy, I'll understand."

"Of course not!" Although surprised by his interest, he also was flattered. "Give me time to make a copy and you can take it with you to read at your leisure."

"Hey, that would be great, since we are leaving tomorrow morning."

Satisfied, Jack stood up and shook Eric's hand in dismissal. "You know where to find us." And they parted ways.

Roxy spent the afternoon with her parents. They ended up at the beach and found that the water temperature was just right. All three joined hands and jumped the waves like they had done when she was a little girl. They went back in time, with all the laughing and screaming when the waves hit them, sometimes knocking them over. Anne and Roxy didn't even give a second thought about the wet hair dripping down their faces. It was just wonderful!

Supper in the dining room found Ted and Nikki joining Roxy and her parents. After another chef's special left them all satisfied, they relaxed over coffee and enjoyed each other's company. Anne and Jack had waited a long time to have just such a relationship with their daughter and they wanted it to linger a while longer.

Looking at his watch, Ted said that he was on in ten minutes, so they all moved to the lounge. They hadn't been seated very long when Eric and Eileen wandered in and joined them. True to his word, Eric had a box with his novel copied for Jack.

"Let me reimburse you for this, Eric. This will make great reading for me on some of the long plane trips I have to take."

Eric refused his offer and still felt a little self-conscious about sharing his writing with someone he'd just met. *Maybe Jack thought that I would be flattered that he wanted to read my work,* Eric reasoned. And so, he handed him the box and sat down for the piano concert.

Anne watched her daughter's face as she sat with them and listened to Ted play. Even though Ted was playing, his eyes were on Roxy and the mutual admiration they displayed amused both Anne and Jack. She also couldn't help but notice a change in the relationship between Eric and Eileen. Eric's hand was over hers on the table and their chairs couldn't be any closer. Anne looked at her husband and wished that this feeling was contagious. They didn't see too many loving couples in the business crowd they associated with back home. Flirting seemed like a game that was played too often among that group. Anne trusted Jack, but she wasn't blind to the many women who played up to him. When he had to fly out anywhere, he always invited Anne to come along, and sometimes she did, but his meetings left her alone too often. Seeing these happy couples and their devotion to one another created a sharp contrast to their associates, who seemed self-absorbed and superficial. It was a pleasure being with these new friends who made her feel so welcome.

"Jack, would you ever consider looking for property up here? Even just as a get-away place in the summer, it would be wonderful to come and unwind from the fast-paced life we lead. It's certainly healthier, too. That fresh air is stimulating." She looked at him like she had just made a fascinating discovery.

Jack never dreamed these thoughts were in Anne's head. He too, felt so much better where all his worries seem to disappear in the sea air. In fact, this whole day had been a day he would treasure for a long time.

"No, hon, I never have thought about it until now. On my next trip up here, I'll definitely take a look around with that in mind. It's certainly something to think about," he added.

And at the same table, Eric and Eileen had their own plans to discuss. The community college where Eric taught was only a half hour away, so they were already planning for him to spend his weekends and nights in his cottage. It would no longer be just a summer retreat, but a permanent home.

Against the backdrop of Ted's romantic music, both couples considered life-changing plans at their little table.

When Monday morning came, Jack and Anne said their good-byes and promised to return soon. They left Roxy standing there looking forward to their next visit and realizing how lucky she was to have such caring parents. Now her thoughts turned to Ted, as this was his day off and she had plans. Ted had waited patiently for Roxy to have private moments with her folks. Now, it was their time.

"Why don't you come up to my room, Ted, where we can have some time just for ourselves?"

That sounded very promising to Ted.

Once in her room, Roxy sat on the side of her bed and patted the spot next to her for him to join her. His heartbeat quickened as he sat next to Roxy. Without saying a word, she threw her arms around him and pushed him down on the bed and kissed him in a long, passionate kiss. As if he wasn't aroused enough, she reached down and unzipped his pants. Immediately, Ted took over the job while she undressed. The sunlight coming through the window created a silhouette of her body that he had not seen before. He reached his hand out for her arm and brought her towards him in a tight embrace. He needed no directions as his hands were all over her responsive body. Roxy was panting and moving like she had shifted into third gear without going through first and second. This excited Ted, making it extremely difficult for him to have control. He had a hard time saying, "Slow down, hon, or it will end too soon." Knowing he was right, Roxy rolled off of him and let him take the lead.

Ted taught her to enjoy the foreplay, which was a surprise to her. He made love tenderly and in a way that Roxy had never experienced before. She was so convinced that she would be teaching Ted and here he was teaching her the way lovemaking should be done. Her love for him now knew no bounds. He had thrilled her, and she snuggled against him when it was over, listening to his soft words of love for her. Ted adored her and he had shown her his feelings.

"I'm in love with you, Roxy. I have never said that to a girl before. Will you be my girl, hon?"

"What do you mean, 'Will I?' I'm already your girl, silly." She said this while placing her hand on the side of his cheek and giving him a light kiss.

After they dressed, Roxy had a new idea about how to spend their time together. She thought it would be fun to drive down to the marina and rent a boat. It sounded like a good idea to Ted, too. They found a small boat and Ted helped Roxy inside. He climbed in, faced her and picked up the oars. Ted liked seeing Roxy relax and allowing him to take charge.

When they had traveled downstream for a while, Ted put down the oars and anchored the boat. He carefully balanced his way to sit beside Roxy. He had just managed to sit down when she leaned over and kissed him. It was typical Roxy! Ted put his hand under her chin and smiled down at this impulsive girl.

"Roxy, I'm so glad that you care for me, because I'm just crazy about you."

Now that they were away from their music business, she wanted to hear all about her new boyfriend. Ted laughed as he told her about his childhood in a small town where everyone seemed to know everyone else. This knowledge kept most of the kids on the right track. He played baseball in the Little League and won a merit badge in the Boy Scouts. When he tried to tell her that he was just an average boy, she disagreed. To Roxy, he was special. She encouraged him to keep on talking, and he did.

Finally, Roxy suggested that Ted relax and she would row them back to the dock. When she stood up to change places, she started to lose her balance and Ted quickly reacted by jumping up and putting his arms around her. This caused them both to fall back in the boat and land on the floor laughing as the boat steadied in the water.

"Roxy, what is it with you? Maybe you should stay away from boats! You certainly gave me a scare."

She was still laughing when she said, "Would you believe when I was a little kid, I once thought about joining the circus, but I see now that I never would have been able to walk a rope!" They both agreed to that.

Over the next week, Jack spent evenings reading Eric's novel. He hadn't expected to find it so engrossing. It was difficult to stop reading and he was not an easy man to please. Now, he knew what he had to do for Eric.

Jack had an acquaintance in the publishing business who had engaged Jack to sell one of his homes and find him another more upscale place. He had been more than satisfied with the results and Jack remembered him saying, "I owe you one, Jack." Now, he wanted to see if those words held true.

When Bill Bartlet answered the phone, Jack said, "Bill, Jack Rehan here. How've you been?"

"Jack, my man. I'm great! So what's on your mind?"

"Look, I know you are swamped with manuscripts to read but I would really appreciate it if you could read a novel written by an English professor I know. No strings attached, Bill. If you don't think it has merit, just send it back. I will understand and respect your expertise."

"I know you wouldn't ask unless you really did think it was pretty darn good, Jack. And besides, I owe you one. Send it and I'll get right on it. No problem!"

"You're a good friend, Bill. Many thanks. I have a feeling that you're going to be pleasantly surprised." With that he hung up and breathed a sigh of relief.

Two weeks later Jack Rehan received a phone call: "Jack, this is Bill Bartlet getting back to you."

"Bill, what did you think?"

"I'll tell you, Jack, quite frankly I wasn't expecting to find anything special since the novel was written by an English professor; certainly nothing down-to-earth. Was I ever wrong about that! The story really caught my attention. It's so unusual. It starts out as a light mystery and switches to a captivating romance. I could swear that the guy fell in love half way through his story and decided to go with his strong feelings. Hey, whatever happened, it worked. I'll need to speak with this Eric Ames and give him the good news."

"I just knew his writing was exceptional and I'm so happy to hear you agree."

With that, Jack told him how the professor could be reached. Roxy had given her father his private phone number, hoping that it would bring surprisingly good news. Jack could finally come up with a way to repay Eric for all he had done for his daughter.

On Ted's day off he arranged to take Roxy for a nearby hike. When she told him that she'd never been on a nature trail, he was amazed. Hiking was one of Ted's favorite things to do – certainly way up there on his list. Once on the trail, he took her hand and led her down the path, which had beautiful trees forming an arch as they walked along listening to the sound of the birds chirping in the foliage. The air seemed fresher after being filtered by the trees. Ted pointed out bushes that he knew from previous walks and they stopped to read the occasional signs identifying others. Roxy was enthralled by this new experience. It was very quiet except for the ripple in a pond and the rustle of small animals scurrying through the fallen leaves.

In time, they came to a bench and decided to sit and take it all in.

"You know, Ted, reading all those poems has opened a whole new world for me. I truly look at everything in a different way, a deeper way. Can you understand what I mean?"

"Yes, hon, I do. Now, we have something special in common. At least, I think that having deep feelings is very important. On a lighter note," he said, "how would you like to go rafting tomorrow?"

"Would you believe I've never gone rafting? What an awesome idea, Ted!" Now, she had two things to be excited about: her nature walk and the thought of going rafting. Life never looked better.

It was no wonder that, come night, it was hard for Roxy to get to sleep. Ted had introduced her to a new way of living and that, to her, was exhilarating. She relived her nature walk, complete with sounds and smells, and finally fell asleep with a smile on her contented face.

The next day, Eric had returned from his morning beach walk to tend to some household chores when he heard the phone ringing.

When he picked up the phone, he was surprised to hear a pleasant, male voice asking if he were speaking with an Eric Ames.

"Speaking. And who, may I ask, am I talking with?"

"This is Bill Bartlet, a publisher in New York City. I'm a friend of Jack Rehan. It seems that Jack was so impressed with your writing that he felt I might be interested in publishing your novel. I read it and agree with Jack on how promising it is. I'm interested in publishing it." He paused and listened for a reaction. "Are you with me so far?"

Eric was stunned. He'd always hoped to publish his work, but knew how remote the possibility was. "Yeah, just trying to digest what you are saying."

"It will be necessary for you to come to New York and speak with my editors. The sooner the better. We need to discuss what changes you could make to get it to where we could publish it."

"That would be great, Mr. Bartlet. Thank you. Right now, I need to sit down and do a lot of thinking about all this." Eric replied.

"Take your time for now, but please make your trip here soon so that we can get on with our plans. I am here until five o'clock, so phone me with your decision. Okay?"

With that, Bill gave Eric his phone number and hung up, leaving Eric shaking his head in disbelief.

Once he had regained his composure, he phoned Eileen and gave her the news. She was just thrilled for him.

"New York City! I just sent my last paintings to my agent for a showing next week. I was going to try and get out of an appearance there so I could stay here with you. If you think you might like company, and could hold off until next week, we could go together."

"Are you kidding? You just made my day, Eileen."

Eileen and Eric made arrangements and flew together to New York. Eileen's agent, Renée Lamere, had allowed her to stay in a guest room at her apartment since Eileen had sold her own place. She mentioned that if Eric wouldn't mind sleeping on a couch, he was welcome, too. They happily decided to accept her offer and forgo the expense of a hotel.

When they arrived in the city, Eileen gave Eric directions to the art gallery and then he left for his meeting with Bill Bartlet's editor. Once there, he felt that the book discussion went well and he agreed with the few changes the editor suggested. After signing a contract, he took a cab to the gallery.

Although the gallery was unimpressive from the outside, the interior was attractive. He found Eileen busy placing the paintings in groups according to the subject matter and helping Renée hang them. Eric was impressed with the large number of canvases she had painted in the short time since her last showing. Her particular style was evident in each one.

Eric carefully studied each painting, and was in awe of her extensive talent. There were many seascapes, but also landscapes, still lifes, and a few portraits. Eileen smiled as she watched his serious face so deep in thought.

"Well, what do you think? Did I win you over?"

"In more ways than one," he answered with a sly smile. "Even if I didn't know the artist, I would be an added name on your list of fans."

"That means a lot to me, Eric." She looked at her watch and announced, "We open at seven tonight and I'd like you to be here with me. I'm really not good at small talk, but if they want to discuss style or subject matter, well, that's fine by me. There will be a few collectors of my paintings and I enjoy talking with them, and I am flattered to know that they still want to add to their collections. Anyway, that is what you can expect if you join me tonight."

"Wouldn't miss it for the world!"

He, too, looked at his watch and said, "Are you about ready to break for dinner?"

"You read my mind. We'll put out the wine and snacks just before the patrons arrive." She looked at Renée and said, "We're out of here now. You're welcome to join us for dinner. What do you say?"

"Sounds good to me, Eileen, and we're early enough to get seated at a nice restaurant. Let's wrap it up for now."

Renée was right about not many people arriving before five o'clock, so they didn't have to wait to be seated at the popular restaurant. They were led to a circular booth with soft leather cushioned seats. Eric ended up sitting in the middle with a pretty female on either side of him. He asked to see the wine list and then chose a good bottle of wine. After sampling the bouquet of the wine, he indicated to the waiter to fill their glasses.

"To another successful art showing," Eric toasted and they clicked their glasses and sipped the rich wine.

Renée had put out extensive publicity for the gallery opening and talked about some of the replies she had received. She threw out a few names for Eric to become acquainted with if he wanted to know more about who's who in the art world. Renée wanted him to have a good experience at her gallery. She took her job as hostess very seriously.

They all agreed that their meal was a perfect example as to why the restaurant earned its five stars.

They arrived back at the gallery at six-thirty and began setting up a table of tasty snacks, some fresh fruit, and two punch bowls, one with alcohol.

Just before seven, a few people wandered in and were warmly greeted by Renée. When they spotted Eileen, they rushed over to talk with the artist and to question her about some of the paintings visible from where they stood. Eileen patiently explained why she chose a certain subject and just how her composition was planned. As more and more people came in, there was a small line waiting to talk with her. Renée handled the sales and helped settle a few disputes between two people who wanted the same painting. All and all, the evening went well and Eileen was glad that she'd made the decision to be present, as that certainly influenced the buyers.

Back at Renée's apartment, they discussed the different personalities of the art lovers they'd met at the show. Some had shown up in wild, colorful outfits complete with hats of unusual designs. Most were very complimentary when talking with Eileen and couldn't say enough about this new assembly of paintings. Eric marveled at how humbly Eileen handled all of this, never letting it go to her head. This was just one more trait that he admired in Eileen.

"What do you have in mind for tomorrow?" Eric inquired.

"I am leaving that up to you, Eric. Do you have anything special that you'd like to do?"

"Yes, I do. I guess you know that I am a 'romantic' at heart and since it will be just the two of us, I thought that a carriage ride in Central Park or a ferry boat trip would be fun. Would either one be of interest to you?"

"Oh, Eric! What a great idea! Let's go to Central Park and book a carriage ride. We can have lunch at the Tavern on the Green while we're there. That sounds good to me."

Renée was listening to the two of them excitingly making their plans. She was happy that her friend had met this great guy. She could see they were well suited for each other. She chimed in, "Well, I have a surprise for your evening." She took out two tickets to *Pretty Woman* and handed them to Eileen.

"No kidding, Renée! How in the world did you manage to get them?"

"When you phoned to say that you were coming and bringing Eric, I pulled some strings and was successful. I've seen the musical and was impressed. You'll love it!"

The next day, the weather was just right for their plans. They arrived early for lunch at the popular restaurant. After they were seated and ordered, Eileen surprised Eric with a bit of history.

"Did you know that the Tavern on the Green once housed 200 sheep? That was way back in 1870. You see, it didn't become a restaurant until 1934. Changes were made throughout the years, but it is still here and still popular." Eric was impressed with her story.

After lunch, Eric poked in the gift shop while Eileen went to freshen up. He spotted a small, cardboard box in the image of the restaurant. On a lark, he bought it, folded it and stuck it in his pocket.

After lunch, they climbed into a waiting carriage and started on a leisurely ride through the park.

As they moved along, Eric became serious and looked at Eileen saying, "I planned this ride so that I could tell you what you mean to me. Although we have known each other for only a short time, I can't get you out of my mind, Eileen. I need to know if you have similar feelings about me."

Seeing her shocked expression, Eric took her hand in his and said, "You should know that, to me, this is not just a casual affair that we are having."

The clip, clop of the horse's hooves seemed suddenly louder in the silence that followed Eric's declaration. All this intimate talk made Eileen uncomfortable.

She turned towards him and replied, "Eric, I do have strong feelings for you, but let's just enjoy each other for now and not get so serious."

He squeezed her hand and accepted her answer.

When the driver reached the Bethesda Fountain, he stopped so they could admire its attraction. Once again, Eileen offered some history about the Angel of the Water statue at the fountain.

"The statue refers to the Gospel of John, which describes an angel blessing the Pool of Bethesda and giving it healing powers. This terrace is a nice place to visit, don't you think?"

They rode on to the Bow Bridge which was named because it resembled an archer's bow. Eileen thought it was a good place to take a selfie. The carriage stopped long enough for a few camera shots, and then they moved on, enjoying the sights that the park had to offer.

Chapter 7

Ted was all smiles just thinking about taking his Roxy rafting for her first time. It so fit her personality.

The weather was in their favor: bright and sunny. As they boarded the shuttle van, Roxy asked the names of the other eight people and introduced herself. Once seated, she loudly inquired, "So, how many of you guys are rafting for the first time like me?" Of the eight people, three were new to the experience. The remaining five were a family that had been twice before and were hoping to repeat the thrill of the last two times.

At the rafting station, they were given life jackets and helmets to put on. "I feel like the 'marshmallow man' from *Ghost Busters*," laughed Roxy at the added girth as she hugged her arms around the bulky jacket and did a little stiff-legged dance, much to the amusement of the other people around her. Her crazy antics just endeared her more to Ted.

The family of five boarded the raft with one instructor, leaving Ted and Roxy to board with the remaining three and another instructor. The instructor told them how and where to sit and gave everyone an oar. The instructor also stressed how important it was to tuck their feet under the side of the raft for support and to remember which side they were on. When the instructor shouted, "left forward," those on the left side must paddle forward. Likewise, if the order was "right backwards," those on the right side must paddle backwards. The steering procedure required teamwork from all of them. Roxy liked the idea of being part of a team and took her role seriously.

Roxy was so excited that it was hard for her to contain her emotions as they set out on the river. At first the current was calm, but as the river sloped downward, they sped up and really had to concentrate on the rapid instructions so they could avoid the rocks and try to stabilize the raft.

The wilder the ride, the more Roxy screamed with excitement. "Hot damn! We're flying in this thing!" She paddled furiously with wide eyes, laughing at the cold splashes that were soaking her clothes.

She forced her feet back hard for better support, knocking off her damaged toenail in the process. With Roxy, however, the excitement outweighed the temporary pain in her toe, but as she reached down to check on her foot, she lost her balance and slipped over the side. Ted was horrified and ready to jump in after her, but the instructor threw out a tow rope and pulled her back in.

Other than being soaked to the skin, Roxy was unhurt and laughing, when she said, "Now that was an adventure!" Then she looked at Ted's serious face and said, "Ted, you're white as a ghost! Are you okay?"

"Damn it, Roxy! You scared me half to death." Roxy just laughed and picked up her paddle and continued where she'd left off as though nothing had happened. She loved every minute of it and hated to see it end. The other passengers let it be known that Roxy had made the ride a real adventure and that they'd be back again if they knew that Roxy would be in their raft. Both Ted and Roxy had to laugh at that.

When they got to the car, Ted pulled out a blanket from the trunk and wrapped it lovingly around her. He looked at her toe with the missing nail and shook his head in dismay. She saw the look and said, "Hey, it was dead already from a temper tantrum when I kicked a dresser. It was ready to come off, so no big deal. I'll just paint the skin with nail polish to match the other nails and you won't even know that it is missing."

Again Ted shook his head. "You're hopeless, girl. You know that?" To his way of thinking there was only one Roxy and, thank heavens, he was lucky enough to find her.

Back in New York, the other courting couple prepared for their evening show.

They both looked forward to seeing the popular musical, *Pretty Woman*. Renée had purchased good seats for them and, as expected, the singing, acting, and story moved their emotions through sadness and joy. At intermission, Eric commented to Eileen, "You know, Eileen, I could see your Nikki in a musical."

"Yes, I have to agree with you, Eric, but her chances of that happening are nonexistent. You need experience and training just to audition for a role like that." She smiled approvingly and added, "Nice thought, though!"

Eric was a dreamer and as he sat in the music hall, he tried to visualize his own novel made into a musical. He thought that it must be thrilling when something like that comes to fruition. And then he picked up his program to read about the cast and their backgrounds, and his daydreams disappeared like a fragrant whiff of perfume on a windy day.

When the show ended, they joined the audience in a standing ovation for the cast, which deserved the grand tribute. All the way back to the apartment, the songs replayed in their minds, extending the joy of the evening.

Back in Maine, Jack and Anne Rehan arrived at the inn feeling confident that they were soon going to be a part of this beachside community. Jack had made inquiries and they were about to check out some of the upscale cottages on the market. They invited Roxy to join them, as this would be her home, too. With the economy at a low point, people were scaling down and some of the properties were even foreclosures.

The realtor, Mrs. Hayes, was anxious to unload some of the expensive homes that had been on the market for many months with no hits. The owners were getting nervous and willing to lower the price, which was in the buyer's favor. Although many were suitable houses, they didn't spark Anne and Jack's interest. Finally, Mrs. Hayes showed them a large, well-kept house that was close to the beach, and all three knew that this was the one for them. It even came furnished, as the owners had moved away and wanted to unload the whole package. Roxy's eyes lit up when she saw the glassed-in den with a piano just waiting to be played. She and Ted could work here undisturbed and could better prepare for their recording session.

Mrs. Hayes was excited about the sale, knowing that she would be guaranteed a nice commission and everyone would end up happy. It was a big decision, but they all felt it was the right one for them.

Meanwhile, back at the inn, John was listening to one of his regular customers, Tim, complaining. Tim was the congenial owner of the local playhouse and was finding it hard to make ends meet.

"There are so many repairs that I need to tend to, but the expense keeps rising. It's been a good run, John, but I'm getting too old to take on all these problems. I'm seriously considering selling the place, but who would buy that old building?" He shook his head sadly. "The thought of a stress-free retirement sounds pretty good to me right now." He gulped down his drink and left John with his business mind spiked into full gear.

When Roxy and her parents entered the lounge, it was almost empty. They sat at the bar to tell John the good news. He liked Jack and Anne and was pleased to know that he would be seeing them quite often as owners of their new vacation home. In the course of their conversation about real estate, John told them about the playhouse.

"God, if I only had the money, what I could do with that place. I'd fix it up and bring in some traveling groups and put on musicals." His eyes lit up picturing all his grand ideas materializing. Then he shrugged his shoulders and added, "But, hey, I have all my finances tied up in this place. I'm not sorry, because I've done well, especially since Nikki became our headliner. Without the playhouse, folks around here are going to be looking for some form of entertainment. It's going to be tough!"

Jack took all of this in and asked, "John, if someone bought the playhouse, would you consider managing the bookings and running the place? I imagine you could easily hire a bartender to work here without giving up your interest in the inn."

John looked puzzled and thought a minute. "Well, yeah, sure! I guess I would. But why even harbor such a thought?"

Jack smiled, "Well, since that is my line of business, I might be interested in buying the place as an investment if I thought you could carry out all those plans you just proposed."

John's eyes widened. "You're serious? You really are interested in the old playhouse?"

"That remains to be seen, John. I have to see the owner, look over the place and then put my cards on the table. In the meantime, it's our secret, John. Okay?"

"Yeah, sure! Some secret! Now, I'll be on pins and needles waiting to know how all this turns out."

Roxy's head bobbed back and forth as she listened to each side of the conversation with excited interest. "That's awesome, Dad! Then maybe I could be in one of the musicals, huh?"

"For crying out loud, Rox. Don't you go jumping to conclusions. Just erase all this speculation from your mind and let me handle things. You got that?"

Roxy put on her innocent face and said, "Never heard a word. Not to worry, Dad."

John laughed and wrote down Tim's address for Jack and his hand shook with anticipation of what might transpire from this simple exchange.

Meanwhile, Nikki waited at the airport to pick up Eileen and Eric. As she watched them coming towards her, she realized how lucky they were to have found each other. All the way back home, they chattered on about their marvelous stay in New York.

Eileen and Eric heard that Roxy's parents were staying at the inn. Since they enjoyed their company when they last visited, Eileen and Eric thought they would stop by the lounge in the hopes Anne and Jack might show up. Nikki decided to tag along even though it was her night off.

They had guessed right, and they spotted Anne and Jack having a drink while waiting for Roxy and Ted to arrive. They ended up pushing two tables together to fit everyone near the piano.

Then it was Jack's turn to describe his new house and announce that they'd be living close by. Everyone was in such a good mood that John chimed in with, "This calls for a celebration with drinks on me."

At this point Roxy came in with Ted and they joined the group.

Eric talked about their trip to New York and when the subject turned to the musical, *Pretty Woman*, Roxy perked up and said, "I heard rumors that there may be changes at the playhouse; like maybe bringing in some professional groups to put on musicals right here. Now, wouldn't that be awesome!" Jack's glare cautioned her to go no further. Sometimes he felt like he was trying to plug up a hole in a dam whenever she started spilling out a story. He had to give her credit though; she wasn't actually giving away their secret.

Roxy rambled on, "You know, Nikki, that might be a way for you to audition for a part. They usually look for extras and when they hear your voice, well, you never know, right?"

Nikki admired her enthusiasm over something that was just a rumor. Roxy was always so optimistic. It was part of what made her so endearing to Nikki.

"First, we have to get that recording done, Roxy, before we make other plans. How close are you and Ted to finishing that last song?"

It was Roxy's time for good news. "Ted and I have it ready for you to practice, Nikki, and we kept your voice in mind as we worked on it. It's tailor made for you. Now, it's up to you to give it that final touch that only you can do. After that, we can book our recording date."

"Sounds good to me. Let's go for it!"

As for Jack, he decided to get on with his plans by starting with a trip to the playhouse. Once there, he liked what he saw and could see the possibilities that John had talked about. Over the course of the next three weeks, Jack was able to negotiate with Tim and plans were drawn up for a large extension to the back of the building to accommodate an orchestral pit and more dressing rooms. A new roof would have to cover both the old and the new building. All these expenses were tallied up when Jack made his offer and Tim liked his ideas and his generous offer.

Jack's plan was to keep it open for three seasons of the year, only closing in the winter. He was encouraged when hearing of the success of places like the South Shore Music Circus, where interest in musicals proved popular. He planned on hiring Nikki to help with the marketing end of the business. He hoped to start paying off his huge investment once they became known. Anne never interfered with any of his business transactions, but he knew she didn't share his enthusiasm about this venture. Much too chancy to her way of thinking.

Nikki was a quick study, and when she sang the songs for Ted and Roxy, they were thrilled with what she added to the songs' appeal. She instinctively knew when to soften her voice or give it her all and the result was beautiful shading that enhanced everything that Ted and Roxy had written beyond anything they had expected.

"I can't believe we made such beautiful music! This is going to make one hot recording." Roxy was finding it hard to contain herself and her optimism was contagious.

The trio went ahead with the recording. When it was finished to their satisfaction, they brought it to the Boston disc jockey to see if he would keep his word about listening to it. Once he had heard it, he looked at these three amateurs in amazement.

"Well, I'll be! You did it! When I suggested your making this recording, I thought it would be something fresh and appealing, but the result is far beyond what I was expecting. Seriously, I really think that you people have a hit here." They left the studio uplifted.

Eric had been traveling to his college every day to prepare for teaching. He was pleased to discover that Roxy had signed up for three of his classes: Creative Writing, Grammar, and Poetry 2. She felt able to handle all three classes after the dedicated hours spent with her summer studies. At first, Eric thought that she might have overextended herself, but she had proven him wrong before, and so he agreed that she probably could manage just fine. He had learned to trust her judgment and, in the process, he discovered a very intelligent young lady.

With Eric away most of the day, Eileen had gone back to spending more hours painting and found that she missed having Eric teaching Roxy in her kitchen. Just knowing they were there had brought warmth to her house.

Most nights Eileen and Eric managed to have supper together, either at her house or dining out. Seeing less of each other actually made their time together more important and completed their days.

Nikki worked with John on promoting the new music hall. Once all the reconstruction was finished, they wanted to have their bookings in place. Jack had complete faith in their endeavors and the high salaries he gave them showed his appreciation.

Meanwhile, Jack anxiously checked into the publishing of Eric's book and found out that it was in the hands of book reviewers before the book released. Jack hoped that their opinions would be favorable. He knew that it was always difficult to get started in this business, no matter how good a writer you were. He had a hunch that Eric would prove to be the exception.

With Roxy all wrapped up in school assignments, Ted had no incentive to compose any new songs. He missed her presence when he played at the lounge and, sadly, Roxy's favorite spot was filled with new faces that showed little or no interest in what he played. The highlight of his life was whenever Roxy could fit in time to be with him and he treasured those moments.

As weeks passed, Roxy proved herself to be an apt pupil. She soaked up everything Eric presented in class. He was always available to help her if the need arose, and he became a surrogate father to her, and a doting one at that.

One afternoon after class, Eric saw Roxy still sitting at her desk deep in concentration. "Anything that I can help you with, Roxy?"

Roxy looked up. "Oh, professor, no, it's just that I want to write to the best of my ability for Ted. His music is so beautiful that it deserves the right lyrics. Ted is an exceptionally gifted man, you know! I feel honored that he accepts an amateur writer like me to collaborate with on his songs."

"Well, Roxy, I think he's the one who should feel honored. You've worked so hard and come so far that I, for one, am amazed at the results of your efforts. You two seem destined to become the next Lerner and Loewe."

Roxy grinned and said, "Wouldn't that be something!"

Meanwhile the work on the music hall was progressing full steam. Jack was able to sweeten the pot and thereby convince the construction workers to work additional hours and complete the reconstruction in record time.

John knew that at this rate, he could book their first musical sooner than planned. With a little luck, he was able to find a touring group doing *Brigadoon* that had an empty slot for two weeks in autumn. He wondered if he dared sign them up before the hall was completed, even though construction was progressing on schedule.

"Now, if this could all just come together nicely, I could sleep nights." John said aloud. He discovered that he had become very fond of his new friends and considered this to be more than just a job. He knew that Nikki felt the same way and that is why she worked so hard to get the word out.

Already the team had transformed the music hall into a first-rate showcase. With Jack's money and John's business savvy, they had done wonders. John's stamp of approval had to be on everything that was done and Jack could be assured that this was all that was necessary.

Nikki was full of ideas, as usual. She suggested to John that they offer discounts on group tickets and contact senior centers all over the state so that they could arrange bus tours to the beach area. John's eyes lit up when she added, "And we could offer discount package tours that included dinner at the inn, followed by the show to complete the experience. That should appeal to all types of clubs, church groups, and community centers, don't you think?"

"I've got to hand it to you, kiddo. You know your stuff. And to think that I was worried about ticket sales."

"That's my job, John. And yes, I do know what I am doing."

The excitement that all this flurry of events generated was infectious. When Jack saw how things were coming along, he no longer questioned his investment strategy. His goal was to see Anne sitting in the front row on opening night with approval flashing in her big smile. He knew of her doubts and yet she always backed him up, so this had to be his payback time to her.

Finally, Jack received the phone call he had been waiting for from Bill Bartlet, the publisher. The critics had given a "thumbs up" for Eric's book.

"It looks like the professor is on his way," remarked Jack.

"He is, indeed. After those reviews, his book will be moving fast. I can guarantee that."

Local newspapers picked up on the news and interviewed Eric. As a result, he soon received invitations for signings at different bookstores, leading to further sales and publicity.

Back at college, Roxy entered her classroom and found a package sitting on her desk. She opened it to find a brand-new novel, *The Changing Heart*, by Eric Ames. Inside was written: "To Roxy, A very bright young lady who taught me a valuable lesson. I discovered that it takes both motivation and good teaching for a student to learn. By working together, we proved that point. It has been a pleasure helping you achieve your goal as a song writer. I wish you continued success. Eric"

Eric was seated at his desk watching Roxy read his note to her. When she had finished, she raised her eyes and gratefully, mouthed the words, "Thank you, Eric." After class, she carefully packed his book in her backpack with plans to start reading it as soon as possible.

That night, Roxy told Ted she couldn't be at her table near the piano, as she wouldn't be able to give her full attention to reading Eric's novel with Ted being so close by.

Roxy decided to read the book while sitting on the bench that meant so much to Eric and Eileen. Here she sat captivated by his tale until the sunset faded the words before her. It was now definitely a romantic novel and Roxy could see bits and pieces of Eric's life interwoven in the story. She even came across one character much like herself. As long as it was complimentary to her personality, she was flattered by the comparison. She took the book home and read most of the night, finding it hard to quit. It gave her satisfaction in knowing that it was because of her dad that the book had been published. Eric had turned her life around and she would be forever grateful.

The next morning, Roxy stayed after class to talk with Eric and relate how much she enjoyed reading his book. Then she asked, "Tell me, did you model your character, Marci, after me, or am I just reading too much into her antics?"

Eric laughed. "So you did notice the similarities? Yes, I tried to capture your exuberance, vitality and sometimes, just plain craziness to give the story a needed lift." He looked at her and tried to guess her feelings. "Did you mind being included in the story?"

"Heck, no. It's nice to know that I can cheer up folks and brighten a few dull lives. At least you can never say that I am boring!"

"That's for sure! I'll tell you one thing, the world could use a few more Roxys around."

As the time for opening night approached, the cast for *Brigadoon* was able to move in a few days early so that they could rehearse with the orchestra. The finishing touches of the hall were being completed during the actual rehearsals. The team knew they were cutting it close, but they were determined to be ready on time.

Tickets were expensive, but still managed to sell well, and three nights were actually sellouts. When opening night arrived, buses came from all over the state, thanks to Nikki's clever advertising. She'd created a website featuring the elegant, newly decorated music hall and the professional cast in full costume.

The first row was reserved for couples: Jack and Anne, Eric and Eileen, John and Nikki, and Ted and Roxy. As the orchestra warmed up, excitement built in the audience. This was true especially for those in the front row.

The curtain rose and the audience fell silent. From that moment on, the cast had a captured audience. The music, the voices, and the story surpassed all expectations.

When it came time for the final curtain call, everyone showed their appreciation by bringing out the actors for many bows.

Jack had his reward when he saw the tears of joy in Anne's eyes. He made sure that John and Nikki were congratulated first, because none of this could have happened without their dedicated efforts. Roxy was jumping up and down until Ted calmed her. To extend the elation, John suggested they celebrate at the lounge.

They ended up at their usual table, reliving parts of the musical and praising the talented singers. It was during the course of this enthusiastic chatter that Roxy spoke up.

"You know, I was just thinking. These musicals all start with a good story. Then they need great music, and then compatible lyrics to carry out the story. Well, what the heck, Eric has a good story, Ted writes great music, and I know how to match lyrics to a story." Her eyes were wide with expectation and she added, "We even have Nikki's voice to pull it all off. Now, is that a great idea or what?"

They all broke out laughing but in the backs of their minds, they wondered if Roxy was on to something plausible.

Eileen spoke first, "Well, I know I may be biased, but I have to say that I think Eric's story would make a fabulous musical!" Again, they all laughed.

Ted turned serious and looked at Roxy. "You know what? Some of the songs on our disc might fit into a romantic story. And if I had Roxy working with me, I could compose other appropriate songs." He gave them a minute to digest what he was proposing, and then asked, "It might be fun trying to do this, Roxy. Want to give it a shot?"

That was all they had to hear. Now the whole group was fired up with this crazy idea. They knew there would be no commitment so, they reasoned, if it never materialized no harm would be done. And too, the songs could go toward another album, which they had been considering doing anyway.

Their emotions were already high from the show, but now, they were even higher. Roxy had a way of always raising people's expectations because she truly believed this was possible. So after another round of drinks, they were all convinced that they should give it a try.

John was already figuring out how he could replace one of the tentative bookings with this proposed musical. Possibly next summer, he concluded, if everything fell into place. Roxy promised Ted that somehow, she would find the time to work with him and they could use the piano at her house. Nikki, having read the book, easily saw the potential for a new musical. Jack concluded that Roxy had, indeed, inherited his business mind and he was bursting with pride just listening to her ideas.

As for Eric, everything was happening at such a rapid pace that it was difficult to remain focused on all the planning that was taking place in front of him. The thought that it was his book that started this rush of ideas placed the responsibility on his shoulders for the success or failure of this musical.

Needless to say, not many had much sleep that night. Nikki was busy thinking of ways to make this dream of Roxy's actually come full circle and end up being performed at the new music hall.

Chapter 8

When their high emotions had settled down a few evenings after that night, Roxy was in the lounge at her usual spot and decided to go to the bar for a refill. Sitting at the bar was a young man of about twenty-five, dressed in designer jeans and a bright colored t-shirt. He had been eyeing Roxy. Now, as she approached the bar to ask John for a drink, the man spoke to her.

"No date tonight? Can I get you a drink?" That seemed to amuse him as he watched her reaction.

"Can't a girl sit alone?" Not waiting for his answer, she continued. "I manage just fine on my own."

He smirked at that. "I'll bet you do! But how do you know what you're missing?"

Roxy glared at him.

"Hey, lighten up, okay? I'm just starting a conversation because I'm alone, too."

"Well, you had your conversation and that explains why you're alone." Roxy picked up her drink and started to leave when he began to laugh at her.

"You're a little fire cracker, aren't you?" Roxy took that as a compliment.

"Yeah, that's me." She said sarcastically and put her drink back on the counter. He saw that as a signal to continue the conversation.

"My name is George and I'm leaving for a beach party I heard is guaranteed to be awesome. Since you are obviously unoccupied, how about joining me?"

Instead of going back to her seat, Roxy sat down next to George. She had to admit that a beach party sounded pretty good to her. Although aware that John was taking all this in, ready to step in if necessary, she hadn't noticed that Ted's playing had become louder as his anger mounted. She was oblivious to his disbelief that she was striking up a conversation with this stranger.

George lowered his voice to a whisper as John hovered near them.

"You know, you look like you appreciate the finer things in life, so I am going to let you in on a secret." Roxy could hardly hear him, making it necessary to move a little closer. She didn't realize she was playing right into his hands.

George put his hand to his mouth so that his voice would be less likely to carry to John's sharp ears.

"I have the best pot in my car that you could ever hope to smoke. This weed is guaranteed to give you the biggest kick you have ever experienced." He paused to let this startling news sink in before he asked, "A full body high! Interested?"

Roxy hadn't smoked pot since leaving the rough crowd that she'd hung around with before coming to the inn. Listening to George brought back memories and she found herself wanting to try his stronger version.

Reading her facial expression, George knew he had a customer. She was a lot easier than expected and he was proud of himself for being such a good judge of character. He gulped down his drink and whispered, "Think about it. I'll wait outside in my car for fifteen minutes. Just remember this stuff will knock you off your feet. I'll even let you sample it free before you decide to buy a bag. That's the kind of guy I am. You'd be nuts to pass up a deal like that!" George got up and left without looking back.

Roxy sat there awhile fighting a strong temptation to sample a few puffs. She missed that old feeling and the urge was overpowering.

John watched her and was troubled by the whole scene.

"What was that all about, kid?"

Roxy looked up with a dazed expression and answered, "Oh, nothing. He was just coming on to me and finally decided to give up. Weird kind of guy, huh?"

Instead of taking her drink back to the table, she drank it there, paid John and left the room.

In the parking lot, Roxy spotted a flashy silver and red car in the back, under a tree, making it hard to find. Figuring he would pick an out of the way area for his shady deals, she hurried so as not to be missed at the lounge.

There sat George with a big grin on his face, puffing on his reefer. Roxy opened the passenger door without returning his smile.

"So, let's see this sample that you talked about."

"Now, you're talking." he said.

He took a long drag from his reefer and then passed it to Roxy. She put it to her mouth and inhaled deeply and waited for the rush. When it came it was, indeed, stronger than anything she remembered, and she missed that sensation.

George reached over and grabbed it back before she realized what he was doing.

"Okay, you had your sample. Now, you can cash up if you want a bag of weed."

She looked in her handbag for her wallet and handed him thirty dollars.

"We are talking top of the line here, girlie. Cough up another twenty and it's yours, And maybe next time I might introduce you to Fentanyl."

Roxy was so anxious for more that she didn't hesitate to give him another twenty. He handed her a small bag. They were both looking down at the bag when the passenger door flew open and there stood John in a rage.

He grabbed Roxy's arm and literally pulled her out of the car. George immediately started up the car and took off before they even closed the door. Roxy had her still open handbag in one hand and the marijuana bag in the other and a stunned look on her face.

John grabbed her arm roughly and yelled at her to hand over everything that she had just bought from George. He was hoping it wasn't hard drugs she was into, and to some extent, he was relieved that it was marijuana.

"Are you out of your mind, Roxy? I'm tempted to have you both arrested. I caught sight of his license plate number, you know. As for why I'm not turning you both in, it's that I believe it was a moment of weakness on your part. Am I right?" he said, giving her an undeserved break.

The only reason Roxy looked upset was because she had gotten caught and he took away the best pot she had ever come across and she really wanted to go to that beach party. Furious at John, she yelled, "Why don't you fuck off, John. Now, I missed out on a beach party, too. Just give me back my bag and I'll smoke it off your premises so no one need ever know."

John couldn't believe his ears. She was even ready to go to a beach party with him! And he had thought that she had turned over a new leaf.

"Why, you ungrateful brat! You just broke the law, gave a pusher your money, and destroyed the faith that Ted and I had in you. I have a good mind to phone the police after all. Your pal needs to be taken out of circulation, but since it would involve turning in you, too, I'm giving you a second chance. But mark my word, Roxy, there will be no third chance. Do I make myself clear?"

Roxy really wanted that bag back, but realized what John said was true. Used to having whatever she wanted, she didn't appreciate having John mess things up. Looking up, she saw Ted standing in the doorway taking in the whole conversation. That really hit home. She loved the guy and right now the look on his face scared her back to her senses. This was a deep hurt that she, alone, had caused him. At that moment, all self-respect was lost and she ran to him in tears.

"Ted, I'm sorry. I don't know what I was thinking. I never meant to hurt you. I can promise you it will never, ever happen again. You mean too much to me. Please try to understand," she pleaded.

Ted had to turn his back on her so that she couldn't see his pain. To his way of thinking, this was not the girl he had pledged to love. He walked sadly back to the lounge without saying a word.

Roxy was horrified. She would have preferred his screaming at her, calling her names, anything but just walking away. Her heart was truly broken.

Sitting down on the stairs, she sobbed and hated herself for the first time in her life. Ted would never understand that with the crowd she used to hang around with, this was nothing but smoking for fun. She had broken the law without a second thought. Ted deserved better and she knew it.

She went to her car and drove home without ever going after Ted. To her way of thinking, "What was the use?"

Ted was at the bar when John came in.

"Ted, Roxy isn't like other girls. That's one of the reasons that you were attracted to her in the first place. True, she shouldn't have bought from a sleazy pusher like that jerk. But, in her mind, smoking pot is no big deal. Try to understand that, Ted."

Ted shook his head in denial. "John, I thought I knew her and I now see that I didn't. I knew that she had a loose past and I accepted that. I thought it was all behind her. Now I see that she's up to her old habits. For all I know, she might have gone off with that jerk to some party if you hadn't stepped in when you did. Did you see how she stayed talking with him? What else had he offered her, John?"

"You're reading much too much into this episode, Ted. I'm certain she just wanted to try the marijuana and that's it."

"Wish I could see it your way, John, but right now, I can't."

John poured him a drink and left him alone.

When Nikki came to rehearse that night, she didn't see Ted. She went up to John at the bar to ask where Ted was. John told her the whole story and his take on it.

"Yes, I am worried about Ted, but I am more worried about Roxy. Her emotions are so strong that I don't know what she'll do about losing Ted. I saw the look on her face and felt the love in her heart. Do you suppose you could take a ride over to her place and see if you can help her?"

"Of course I will. I think we all expected too much of that girl. People don't just change from black to white without a gray area in-between. I understand Ted's disappointment, but I agree with you that he's reading too much into the incident."

Nikki left and went straight to Roxy's parent's house, where Roxy had moved, but her car wasn't there. She got out and looked in the large glass windows of the den. She could see piano music thrown on the floor and a bottle of vodka on the end table with a glass on its side next to the bottle.

Knowing that Roxy didn't have a drinking problem, Nikki was scared. She tried to think where in the world Roxy might go to sulk. The first place to come to her mind was the beach.

Once there, she saw Roxy's car parked, but empty. Hurrying to the bench, she stopped and steadied herself and looking toward the water, saw Roxy fully dressed and barefoot. Her shoes were in the sand halfway between the water and the bench. Her handbag was also thrown in the sand. Nikki noticed that she was trying to walk a straight line to the pier with difficulty. She kicked off her own shoes and started running to Roxy, all the while screaming her name. The wind was blowing the sound away, and the breaking waves drowned Nikki's voice from reaching Roxy. The tide was out, making it a long way for her to run. Nikki stumbled and kept on running. By now, Roxy had reached the pier and appeared to be trying to keep her balance as she walked towards the small bench on the end. She had almost reached the bench, when she slipped and fell over the side into the fast-moving water.

Nikki saw Roxy struggling to keep her head up with a look of fear on her face. Just as Nikki reached the water, to her horror, she saw Roxy's head disappear under the waves and not pop up again. Nikki rushed to the water and dove in. She swam to the spot where Roxy went under. The foam blocked her view and she wondered if she had misjudged the area. She looked to see if Roxy had come up for air, but only saw the waves pushing onto the shore. Once again, she dove and swam around until she saw there was something to her right. As she swam closer it was apparent that it was the lifeless body of her friend. She reached out and pulled her up to the surface but there was no gulping of air as she had hoped would happen. Struggling to pull her ashore, Nikki prayed aloud.

"Dear God, please don't let her die."

She laid her on her stomach and tried to pump the water out of her lungs. After some anxious moments, Roxy began to spit up and cough. Nikki found her purse that she had left on the beach and grabbed her cell phone. She called 911 for an ambulance and continued doing what she could for Roxy, who at least was breathing. Nikki cried and called Roxy's name until the ambulance came and took her away to the hospital, still unconscious.

Once inside her car, Nikki phoned her mom first. Eileen found it hard to believe that a tough cookie like Roxy would do something so foolish over a breakup. It crossed her mind that maybe they really didn't know how deep her feelings for Ted had become. Eileen told Nikki that she would meet her at the hospital. Once Nikki had phoned John, she drove home to get out of her soaking wet clothes before heading to the hospital.

When John heard the news from Nikki's phone call, he had tears in his eyes. He had become so fond of Roxy; after all, she was in the lounge just about every day. He knew that she looked up to Ted as a truly decent person and perhaps concluded that she wasn't good enough for him. He was dreading telling Ted.

Nikki sat beside Roxy's bed at the hospital and held her hand tenderly. Although they were so different, Nikki considered her a good friend. The doctor had said that her blood alcohol measured at an extremely high level. He wondered how she had even made it to the beach. There was a good chance that she had passed out and then went under the water. He seemed optimistic about her regaining consciousness soon.

Once again, Nikki called her name and this time Roxy's eyes opened and looking bewildered, she asked, "Nikki? What happened? Am I in a hospital?"

"You drank enough to knock yourself out and then you decided to walk out to the pier. You're very lucky I was there to get you out. Don't go feeling sorry for yourself, Rox. You have to look forward, not backward. Resolve to be a better person and forgive yourself. You have a lot of friends here who will help you through any weak moments. You need only ask. But if it happens again, you're going to need professional help. So, girlfriend, kick yourself in the butt and straighten up so Ted can, once again, see the girl he fell in love with."

Roxy knew that she was lucky to have such a good friend.

Back at the lounge a very upset Ted came in still brooding over Roxy's behavior. John came up to him and told him to sit down because he had some bad news. When he related what had happened, Ted was visibly shaken.

"My God, John. This is my fault, isn't it? I should have answered her when she came up to me. What if Nikki hadn't been there? Never, never, would I have forgiven myself if she hadn't been able to revive Roxy. Oh, John, I have to go to the hospital now."

"Yes, you do, Ted. Good luck!"

Eileen arrived at the hospital with Eric after calling Roxy's parents. They found Nikki consoling Roxy and assuring her that her friends wouldn't condemn her for her foolish act. Eileen hurried to her and hugged her.

"Did you think that all that heavy drinking would help you solve your problems? All it did is make you lose your balance and almost lose your life." Roxy agreed with Eileen that it was a dumb idea.

Eric hugged her, too, and assured her that he was always there for her.

Roxy apologized for worrying all of them and tried to explain that had she been sober, she never would have walked out on the pier to escape her troubled situation. They had to agree with her.

She looked up to see Ted entering the room with a pained expression on his handsome face. When he reached her, all he could get out was her name. Roxy threw her arms around him. Her friends left the room so Ted could be alone with her.

Chapter 9

Henri Broleau was an interior decorator who owned a very successful business in France. He often had Renée ship Eileen's paintings to his studio in Paris, if he liked the photos that Renée sent him via email. He had personally met Eileen on his many trips to the States and had been immediately attracted to her. In the course of his business transactions with her, he had usually included taking her out to dinner. He always looked forward to those occasions and found himself wishing that he had met her before he had married. Henri's marriage lasted only a few years before both partners agreed that it had been an unfortunate mistake and ended it amicably.

Since his divorce, he found his thoughts turning to his past encounters with Eileen. He knew, of course, that she was a widow now and no longer had the New York studio which she had once shared with her husband, the sculptor. Now that they were both free, he wondered if a more personal relationship were possible.

He phoned Renée and said that he would be in the States and needed to discuss some special-order paintings with Eileen at her new studio in Maine. Henri was a wealthy client and continued to do business with Renée through the years. He was a charming man with a discerning eye for choosing just the right decorative piece of art for his trusting clients. She gave him Eileen's phone number, knowing that Eileen would give a reference commission to her for any purchases that Henri should make. Renée also gave him Eileen's address and told him that her studio was in her Maine home. Henri liked that idea and decided to surprise her with his visit.

By booking a one-way flight into Boston, he was free to extend his stay in Maine if all worked out as he anticipated. He planned on visiting a few art galleries on his return from Maine to Boston, which he felt would work out well for him. After renting a car, he drove to Maine, arriving with high hopes for a new and stronger relationship with Eileen. After a few inquiries, he found her house and decided to surprise her. Eileen came to the door in her artist smock with her paint brush still in her hand and a puzzled expression on her face as she inquired, "Henri! What in heaven's name are you doing up here?" Her expression revealed he was the last person she had expected to see.

Henri knew that he hadn't shown good business manners in not phoning her first for an appointment, but he was still hoping for a happy greeting.

"Don't panic, Eileen. I am here to discuss some painting orders with you personally and I wanted to surprise you." He looked at her paint splattered smock and added, "Now, I see that it must be bad timing. Sorry about that, Eileen. If you're recovered from my blunder, may I come in?"

She stood in the doorway clearly shocked at his unannounced visit. Looking at him reminded her that there was a time, before her marriage, when she was attracted to this friendly Frenchman, but she had known that he was a married man back then.

"Yes, of course, come in, Henri! And yes, you should have phoned me first so that I wouldn't have met you with paint all over me and a brush in my hand."

Henri was relieved that he detected no anger in her voice.

She pulled out a kitchen chair and said, "Henri, sit here a moment while I clean up a bit and then we'll talk. There are some muffins in the bread basket, so help yourself. I'll be back and make us some coffee." With that, she hurried back to her studio and cleaned the paint from her hands and her brushes and hung up her smock. She was still a bit miffed about his unexpected visit.

Henri munched on one of Eileen's homemade muffins while looking around the tastefully decorated kitchen. He expected her to live in a home just like this one. Nice! By now, he figured that she had adjusted to being a widow and since he'd never had a problem attracting the ladies, his spirits were high.

Eileen came back to the kitchen and prepared the coffee, wondering why he had come all this way to discuss business that was usually done at Renée's.

"I heard that you were quite the cook, Eileen." He held up the half-eaten muffin. "Now, I can verify the fact."

"You didn't come all this way to taste my muffins, Henri! So tell me what is on your mind."

He felt her discomfort and wanted to clear the air.

"Business and pleasure both are what is on my mind, Eileen. I will come right to the point."

"Please do."

Henri flashed his big smile. His French accent, with that deep voice, brought back old memories and old feelings. No, Eileen hadn't heard about his divorce, although she knew that it was an unhappy marriage. Nor was she aware of his strong interest in her. She found the whole situation very awkward. Eileen got up for refills of coffee and changed the dynamics of the narrative.

"Henri, before you go on any further, I must tell you that in the last few months, I've met a gentleman and we are seeing each other."

There. Certain that she had set things straight, she now hoped they could get on to the business end of his visit.

Henri stopped the muffin he was holding midway to his mouth.

"Mon Dieu, Eileen! You are not serious, no? Maybe just good friends, right?"

"Yes, we are very good friends, who enjoy each other's company, Henri!"

Henri put his hand to head, "I took it for granted that you were free, Eileen. My mistake."

They both sat there sipping their coffee when he looked up at her with sad eyes and said, "He's a lucky guy, Eileen. I really mean it."

Still she didn't speak.

"In my mind, I still have a chance to compete." He watched her reaction and noticed her smile.

"Oh, Henri, you never were one to give up easily and that's why you have done so well in your decorating business. You are a charmer, and if I hadn't met Eric, I would probably have been interested. However, I have met him, and I do intend to restrict my dating to Eric."

She poured some coffee and continued, "Now that the personal side of your visit is settled, let's get on with the business side."

"Ah, ma belle, you know how to break a man's heart." He shook his head and then took out an envelope of photos.

"These are photos of a few rooms that could use your paintings to complete the right look." The first room had plain, green walls. The furniture was covered with a coral and green pattern and on the wooden floor was a large, oriental rug which picked up the same coral and green. There were black end tables with gold oriental decorations on them. Eileen looked at the photo and suggested carrying out the oriental theme in a couple of large paintings, each displaying an outdoor scene showing a small half bridge and other figures in a pagoda. Perhaps four feet tall by two feet wide. Kimono-clad ladies with fans could incorporate the color theme of the room. Henri agreed that her idea would give a needed symmetry with that design.

Showing her other photos, he discussed color and design with her to fit each setting. Then he placed a big order with her and she hoped that his customers would like the results. While it was fun to create a painting specifically for a room, she preferred painting whatever she liked and having customers select from her completed canvases.

Henri put away the contracts after they were signed and prices agreed upon. After leaving the photos with her for reference, he stood and looked at his watch and said,

"It is 4:45 and I can't think on an empty stomach. For old time's sake, let me take my friend out to dinner."

Henri looked at her with such a hopeful, beguiling look that Eileen had to laugh. She knew that Eric was eating at the college and attending a board meeting that night, so she was free to join Henri if she chose to do so.

"You are a hard man to say no to, Henri. Sometimes I think that you don't know the meaning of the word. I'll tell you what, there's an inn close by that has a wonderful chef who can match your Parisian chefs. My daughter sings at the lounge there twice a week and she is in and out of the place.

Maybe we'll catch her stopping in the dining room and I can introduce you to her. I am warning you ahead of time because her eyebrows will go up if we are seen together. There are two reasons why I am suggesting this restaurant: first, because it has the best food around, and second, so that everything is on the up and up. I don't want anyone thinking that we are sneaking off together on some kind of date. This way, they'll know you are a client."

Henri was amused by her rationale. "Good thinking, Eileen. Let's go and check out this famous chef and I will give my personal assessment."

When they went into the dining room, a French waiter, Pierre, asked to serve their table when he heard the pronounced French accent as Henri spoke to Eileen. Pierre's parents were from France and he knew Parisian French.

Once at their table, Pierre suggested a good wine and Henri agreed. He asked if the chef had a specialty and Pierre named a few including his own personal favorite, beef Bourguignon. Henri knew that this dish would take quite a while to prepare, which would give him more time with Eileen. "Yes, that would be fine, and while we are waiting, we will have two bowls of the celeriac Vichyssoise."

"A man of excellent taste, if I do say so myself."

When Pierre came back with their soup, he struck up a conversation with Henri. They ended up talking about different cities in France each had visited and also where some of Pierre's relatives lived.

Eileen watched as Henri won over this young waiter as he always managed to do with people he met. When Pierre left, Henri said, "Eileen, I'm sorry that you were left out of the conversation. Pierre knew my homeland and that is a source of pride to me. You will excuse me, yes?"

"I enjoyed watching his face as he realized that you knew where his relatives lived. You made him very happy, Henri."

"That's good, yes? Now, tell me about this daughter of yours. You say that she is a singer?"

Eileen loved talking about her talented daughter and so she went on to relate how Nikki had majored in marketing and now worked for Jack Rehan, launching the new music hall. When she noted how Henri was genuinely interested, she continued to expand on the big plans they had for this new venture.

Henri loved listening to her and watching the excitement play in her expressions. She was such a joy to be with that there was no way he would give up his efforts to win her over.

In time, their dinners arrived and, true to the buildup, the meal was delicious. As they were eating, Nikki stopped in and did a double take when she saw her mom with this new gentleman. An explanation was in order, for sure.

Eileen looked pleased when she saw Nikki coming to their table. "Oh, good, my daughter has just come in, so you'll get to meet her, after all."

"Nikki, I am so glad that you stopped in as I want you to meet a client and friend of mine. This is Henri Broleau, who has just arrived from Paris." He stood and shook her hand.

"Enchanté, Nikki. I have heard so much about you."

Henri pulled over another chair for Nikki and said, "You will join us, yes?"

"I certainly will. I want to hear about what you do in Paris, that beautiful city I plan on visiting someday."

Eileen knew that her daughter had struck a chord with that announcement. Henri was beaming and, after placing an order for Nikki, he talked about his life in Paris. The two women found his stories delightful. He had them laughing about assignments that went wrong, like the time the wrong paint had been delivered to the workmen and the walls ended up a startling shade of Kelly green. Before he could correct the mistake, the owners came in and, instead of being shocked by the color, had loved the unique, new look to the drab room. He ended up having to work around the color, using a contemporary style that incorporated a touch of the horrible green in the furnishings.

The meal stretched on with humor, bringing on laughter as Henri kept their interest. When they finally got up to leave, Henri said to Nikki, "You must come to Paris and look me up. I will personally escort you on a tour of my beloved city. Promise me you will come, Nikki."

"That sounds great, Henri. If I ever get there, I will indeed look you up."

"I shall look forward to seeing you in my city."

"If you ladies will excuse me, I will see if there is a room available for me at this inn. I had planned on stopping at a hotel I passed with a vacancy sign out front, but this would be a much nicer place." He started to leave when he turned and said, "Wish me luck."

When he was out of sight, Nikki looked at her mom with wide eyes.

"Wow, mom! He comes on strong!"

Eileen laughed and agreed that Henri had a way with the ladies.

"I wonder if he had expected me to offer my guest room to him while he is here. Under the circumstances, that would be inappropriate."

Nikki looked puzzled. "What do you mean by that, Mom? You are such a good hostess that I would have expected you to invite him to stay at our place."

"It's a long story, Nikki. Suffice it to say that the torch is still burning and I need to put it out."

"Are you telling me that he has a romantic interest in you?"

"Yep, that is exactly what I am telling you."

"No kidding? And what are your feelings towards him?"

"Right now, I'm totally confused. I have to admit that I really enjoyed being with Henri this evening. Every time I've ever been with him, he has been as charming as you saw him today."

Henri was heading toward them with that winning smile on his face. "I am in luck, my dears. I will be staying here at this delightful place."

He looked at Nikki and added, "And that means that I will get to hear you sing, ma chérie."

"I will have to sing a French song in your honor."

"Merci. Such a nice memory I shall have to take home with me."

They left the dining room and Henri asked if they would like to go to the lounge for a drink. Eileen needed to be away from Henri to do some serious thinking, so she rejected his invitation. He drove her home and raved about her lovely daughter, all the while hoping for an invitation to stop inside for a drink, but Eileen was quick to exit with, "Thank you for a pleasant evening."

Eileen's emotions were all stirred up. She loved Eric, this was true; but did she love him enough to exclude being in the company of other men? She had to admit that she had a wonderful time in Henri's company. He was so much fun to be with and all his stories held her interest. She really wanted to be with him again because he was so exciting. Eileen found herself wondering what it would be like to date this man and was flattered that he was truly interested in her.

When Eileen left for the beach the next morning, it was with a heavy heart. She actually arrived later than usual because she dreaded the scene to come. Eric was already there and watching her head his way. By now, he felt that he knew her so well he could almost read her mind. The expression on her face puzzled him. Something was up. He just knew it.

"How's my girl this morning?"

"Okay, I guess." Now, he knew something was very wrong.

"Can we just sit on the bench for a while, Eric? We need to talk." He noticed that it was 'the' bench, not 'our' bench.

"Sure, hon, what's troubling you?" He feared her answer.

Eileen told him about Henri in detail: how they met, their business dealings over the years, and how his divorce changed their relationship. Eric listened patiently.

"I can't deny that our time together last night didn't enflame old feelings. This should not have happened. In all fairness to you, Eric, I needed to bring this to your attention."

With a sad look on his face, he said, "I understand that you now have to explore your feelings towards Henri so that you can be sure of what you feel about me. You didn't deliberately try to cheat on me, Eileen. I know that. Our hearts sometimes get thrown a fast ball when we least expect it to happen. I am a patient man and am willing to wait for you, no matter how long that takes." He saw her tears spilling from her eyes.

"Please, Eileen. No tears over this. Hey, you have two guys crazy about you. How lucky can you get?" His attempt to cheer her up only made it more difficult.

"Eric, I really thought I could go to dinner with Henri and keep the client and provider relationship. Had I any idea as to what would happen, I never would have accepted his invitation. But you know, Eric, maybe it's best that I sort out my emotions. Yes, I think I will see Henri a few more times to discover just what went on last night. Maybe it was just the idea of seeing an old friend who was always the eternal optimist. You know, it makes one happy to be with a positive thinking person like Henri. He has a way of making people smile when with them. Perhaps it's just that great feeling that is causing me to be confused." She looked at him encouragingly. "You think?"

"Dear Eileen. Even telling me bad news you manage to say it sweetly. Sure, I'm hurt! I love you. But it is because I love you that I will stand by while you date this Frenchman and explore your feelings." He put his arms around her and she hid her face against his chest.

"If you want to skip our walk today, I understand, Eileen. This has been really hard on both of us."

When she had calmed down, she stood up and said, "If you don't mind, Eric, I would rather go back home." Eileen couldn't remember when she had felt this low.

He kissed her forehead and replied, "It's all right, dear. You go ahead and I'll just stay here for a while."

As she drove off, Eric sat alone on their bench feeling miserable. So he had competition. Well, he would not give up easily. God, he hoped that he wouldn't lose her. Then he got up and walked the shoreline at twice the usual pace while his troubled mind worked overtime.

Chapter 10

Eileen kept ideas in the back of her mind for the rooms pictured in Henri's photos. Although they had briefly discussed what might work for each one, more favorable ideas had since crossed her mind. While it helped to keep busy, she also needed to come to terms with her feelings. She felt that both could be accomplished at the inn, where Henri and she would have other people around them.

When Eileen opened the door at the inn, she heard laughter coming from the dining room. Then she saw Henri and Pierre near the brunch buffet. Pierre looked like he was rearranging the large array of foods just to stall and listen to what Henri was saying. There were also two waitresses putting out more fruit and sweet rolls near where Henri was chatting away. They too, were laughing and looking at him with great interest. Eileen thought Henri was like a magnet the way he drew people to him. It was obvious that he enjoyed being with people and they reciprocated.

He happened to glance up and see Eileen in the doorway. Without hesitation, he called out her name in his loud voice, causing everyone in the room to turn and look at her.

"Bonjour, Eileen. How wonderful that you have come to join me! Perhaps my luck is changing, yes?"

Eileen hurried over to him so that he would lower his voice. Reaching him, she was quick to correct his supposition.

"No, Henri, this is for business, but yes, I will join you."

He handed her a plate and walked with her, suggesting what she might like to eat along the way. Pierre remained near them and nodded in agreement at each suggestion Henri made. Eileen wasn't even hungry, but it gave the two men so much pleasure to have her follow their suggestions that she ended up with a full plate and two happy men.

They brought their plates to the table and Henri announced that he would bring her coffee.

"Is it still, no sugar and one cream?"

Eileen was astounded. "How in the world did you remember that after all these years?"

"That is easy to answer. Because I care about you."

Pierre put out more cream anticipating Henri's next move. Once Henri had prepared their coffees, Pierre helped carry them over to the table where Eileen watched shaking her head in amusement.

Pierre smiled and left them and when they were both seated, Eileen received Henri's full attention.

"I am so happy to see you, ma chérie. Of course, I had planned to visit you today to go over your ideas in detail, but this is so much nicer that you came to see me instead. You perhaps missed me already, yes?"

Eileen was embarrassed by his mistake.

"Henri, it seemed better to conduct business in a public setting and I should have called first. It was a last-minute decision."

"I hope that you will continue to have similar decisions. Such a nice way to start the day today with Eileen sitting in front of me. Ah, if only every day could start this way!" He smiled and added, "I dream a lot, yes?"

Not wanting to encourage him to continue along the same vein, Eileen decided to lead in a different direction by saying, "They have a great selection of good food for brunch,

Henri. In truth, I haven't sampled it but one other time. I think I'll drop by more often."

The small talk didn't divert his attention, and Eileen felt she should let him know where things stand.

"I think that you should know that I have told my friend, Eric, about my having dinner with you last night. It's only fair that he should be aware of our friendship and he was very understanding."

"Really? So does that mean if we go out again, he will keep on being understanding?"

"Please, just let it go. I don't care to discuss it any further. I don't owe you any explanation. So either we change the subject or I will leave."

Immediately, Henri was remorseful. "Pardon, Eileen. So we will talk business like good friends and maybe romance will come later, yes?"

"Henri, you are hopeless. Now, about those photos…" Eileen spent the rest of the breakfast telling him about optional plans, not wanting to start her sketches until being certain she had the final selections.

When they were ready to leave, Henri seemed reluctant to end their meeting.

"Eileen, I have never been in this area before and it would seem only proper that you would be my guide like a good hostess. This is what I will do when you come to Paris." He watched her to see how this settled with her.

"I'd like to take a dip in the ocean and ride the waves. It is such a hot day that you will be refreshed when you join me, yes?"

He had caught her off guard and a dip in the ocean really didn't seem too personal. Maine was enjoying an unusually hot Indian summer this autumn. The beach would be crowded so what would be the harm?

"Well, I suppose I could go for a short time, Henri. But then, I have to get back to my painting if you want me to work on the samples for you to approve."

Henri couldn't believe his luck.

"I will change into my swimming trunks and grab a few beach towels from Joanne, the chambermaid."

"Lord," thought Eileen, "already he knows the name of the chambermaid!"

"I will pick you up in twenty minutes. That should give you enough time to put on your suit and robe. Don't forget to put some sunscreen on your delicate, white skin."

Again she shook her head and rolled her eyes.

True to his word, in exactly twenty minutes, he was knocking at her door. Out came Eileen in a rose-colored, terry cloth robe over a two-piece bathing suit of the same color. The top was a T-shirt style that covered down to the upper half of her shorts so her midriff wasn't exposed. It was too windy to wear a hat, so her hair blew free in the breeze. It was obvious that the outfit met with Henri's approval.

"Ah, a true bathing beauty, Eileen!"

It was late morning and a crowded time at the beach. They had to walk past the bench, but Eileen avoided looking at it, not trusting her feelings. They continued to walk towards the water and placed their beach towels on the sand. Henri slipped off his designer top to reveal his muscular, tan chest. Eileen couldn't help but admire his athletic physique. She noticed a few young ladies nearby watching him as he kicked off his sandals and proceeded to help Eileen take off her robe. He kissed the nape of her neck before she could object.

"Henri, what are you doing?"

"Do you really expect me to ignore your lovely neck when it is kissing distance from me? You ask too much, I think." He took her hand and pulled her toward the ocean before she had time to stop him.

Once at the water, he kept going deeper all the while pulling her along with him.

"Henri, it's cold! Let me adjust to the temperature, will you?"

"Sorry, Eileen. I will jump in first while you get used to it." With that, he disappeared under the waves. When he came up his dark brown hair was no longer slicked back. He looked even more handsome and it was hard not to be physically attracted to this vivacious man.

"You have to join me now. Once you are all wet, you will forget that it is cold. Hey, if you are still cold, you have a nice, warm Frenchman right here to warm you. What more could you ask, right?"

Eileen took a deep breath and dove under the water. She didn't like the cold, so it had been over a year since she had gone all the way into the ocean. When she came up, Henri put his arms around her.

"Nice, yes?" He hoped that she agreed. She wiggled out of his arms and swam away. Henri was a strong swimmer and was beside her before she knew it. After following the shoreline until she tired, they stood up.

"You are a good swimmer, but kind of a slow poke, I think."

They both laughed and she knew that he had figured out that this was something that she didn't do very often.

"Back home, I try to swim as many times as I can fit it into my schedule. It is the best exercise and so enjoyable. Now that you have rested a bit, we ride the waves, yes?"

The waves were perfect for riding and they tried to ride them back to their starting point. By now they were tired enough that the waves threw them off balance and they began giggling like school kids. Eileen would just start to stand when another big wave would start to knock her down again, but Henri's strong arms supported her and she didn't resist. When it was time to go back to rest in the sun, she was still laughing as he put his arm around her and helped her adjust to the rocky areas under her feet as they walked to their towels.

They fell on the towels and used some clean ones to wipe their face and dripping hair. Eileen hadn't felt this free in ages. She had no makeup on and no set hairstyle, yet Henri was looking at her like she was perfectly groomed. She had known Henri for years, but in a guarded way. He was her client and although they always enjoyed their time together, they both were careful to keep the business end alive. Now that they were free to explore other feelings, they were experiencing a newfound joy.

"You know, you were right, Henri. I get so wrapped up in my work that I forget how to let loose and unwind. That was great fun and yes, like you said, refreshing."

"See, you just have to listen to me, Eileen, and I will solve your problems."

He took her back home after she declined his invitation to lunch. She insisted that she had to get started on the samples for him and needed to be alone. Reluctantly, he left.

Eileen propped up the first photo so that she could keep referring to it for inspiration. Next, she took out her sketch pad and charcoal and tried a few small scenes with an oriental theme. After a few hours, she went to the kitchen to make some tea. It was then that the doorbell rang and Eric appeared with a hopeful look on his face.

"Am I allowed in or must I wait until you clear up your indecision?"

Eileen still had salt in her hair and didn't feel presentable, but she couldn't refuse Eric.

"Of course, come in, Eric. I was just making some tea and you can join me if you wish."

"I wish," he answered.

"You know that I can't stop thinking about you, Eileen. It's hard to do anything when my mind isn't on my work. I just had to stop by and see how you were feeling."

"If you mean, have I solved my problems, the answer is no. I'm being up front with you, Eric, when I say I enjoy the man's company. I feel like I'm on a merry-go-round and I don't know when it will stop. All I can say is, please be patient with me because I am totally confused." Then she decided to clear the air even further.

"I do want to talk to you about a problem that I foresee coming up. Henri has expressed his plans to be at the lounge this Saturday night to hear Nikki sing. Now, if you still want to come and meet him, I have no objections, even though I'll be uncomfortable with the two of you at the table. If you'd rather skip our usual Saturday night gathering, I'll understand that, too. Either way, I'm sorry that I put you in this unfortunate situation."

"Wow! That's a dilemma, Eileen! I wasn't expecting that kind of a choice to be asked of me! You know, don't you, that I'll want to tip his chair over with him in it?" He smiled at her hoping to lighten the atmosphere. "I guess curiosity will win over and I'll join you just to see what the competition is like. Is that what you were expecting?"

"Right now I am so embarrassed I have no idea what I was expecting. I have to admit, you're a brave man to subject yourself to scrutiny by Henri."

"Well, I do feel like I'm being put to a test!" he laughed.

"Don't joke about it, Eric. I'm serious."

"Me, too."

"Since you're here, would you like to see what I am doing for Henri?"

"You are referring to paintings, right?"

"Please, Eric! Yes, I am referring to paintings."

She took him into the studio and showed him what she had been working on and she could see he liked what he saw. When she was finished showing him her ideas, he started out of the room but stopped and turned to ask,

"I don't suppose you'd like to go out to supper with me tonight?"

"I just can't, Eric. Sorry. I will see you tomorrow night at the lounge and if you back out it is okay. I won't blame you; only myself."

When Nikki came home to supper, she saw that Eileen was still troubled.

"Did the Frenchman get to you, Mom?"

"If you mean did he win me over, I just don't know how to answer that. We went swimming at the beach and I had a marvelous time, yet I am sorry that I did. Isn't that crazy?"

"After meeting him, I can understand how that happened. Do you know that in just the few days he's been at the inn, everyone there knows who he is? I was asked if I'd met Henri. He talks to everyone and knows all about each and every one of them. Honestly, I don't know how he does it, especially in such a short time."

Eileen proceeded to tell her about Eric's plan to meet Henri at the lounge and sit at the same table.

"Are you serious, Mom? Is that fair to Eric? Are you forgetting your original commitment to this man?" Nikki couldn't go along with doing anything to hurt Eric.

"I know. I know. I feel rotten about the whole thing, but what do you suggest?"

"Well I know one thing—if I were going to a party, I would pick Henri. But if I were to get engaged, I would pick Eric." She saw the tears in Eileen's eyes. "Sorry, Mom, I can't help you this time."

Too soon Saturday night arrived and Eileen was extremely nervous. She wished she didn't have to go, as it was all so cruel to Eric, and he certainly didn't deserve to be treated so shabbily. She hadn't been able to eat much for supper. When looking over the dresses in her closet, nothing appealed to her. Finally, she chose a soft, blue lace dress and she took out a blue sweater for her shoulders in case they turned up the air conditioner. She added her low black pumps and black handbag to the outfit. She twisted her hair up and placed a jeweled clip to fasten it in place. Looking in the mirror she said aloud, "Well, that will have to do, you Jezebel."

Eileen arrived early so that she could prepare Henri for Eric's arrival. At this point, she wanted to forget both men and go home. When she arrived at the lounge, Henri was at the bar and John was laughing so hard you could hear him across the room. When she reached the bar, John greeted her loudly.

"Well, I've been enjoying your client, Eileen. Would you believe, he just talked me into going to Paris and having him escort me around. He should have been a travel agent. Do you want your usual, Eileen?"

She nodded and Henri was looking her up and down with a big grin.

"Très jolie, ma chérie. I will be the envy of every man here."

Eileen ignored his compliment and picked up her drink.

"Come with me, Henri, and I will introduce you to Ted, the pianist. I like to sit by his piano."

Henri followed saying, "Oh, I have met Ted and he is a very talented fellow."

Eileen almost felt angry. "Is there anyone you haven't met, Henri?"

"Yes, Ted's partner in the composing business. He calls her Roxy."

"Well then, you are in for a treat. She is sure to be at our table tonight."

Once seated, Eileen decided to get the announcement over with once and for all.

"And there is someone else who will be sitting at our table tonight."

"By the look on your face, I would say it is someone I won't want to meet."

She cautiously announced, "I have asked Eric to come and meet you and I hope that you aren't opposed to that idea."

"So, I will get to meet your sweetheart in person, Eileen. This is rather awkward, no?"

"Yes, but I didn't want it to look like you were taking his place, sitting here where he is every Saturday night. Does that make sense to you?"

"No, but it's all right. I deal with people all the time so I will try to make him comfortable, so he won't punch me in the nose. Will that make you happy?"

"Now, you have me even more confused. Let's all try to be civil to one another and enjoy listening to Nikki sing. I have explained to Eric that you wanted to hear her and this was your chance. Can you set aside any hostile feelings and just concentrate on her singing?"

"You can count on me, Eileen. I will not make waves. So when does Nikki start singing?"

"You'll see this place fill up before Nikki walks in. But she does know that you are here especially to hear her sing so, who knows, she may come early just to visit with you."

"I'd like that."

No sooner had he said that when Nikki came in and right to their table.

"Hey, guys, glad you could make it! Roxy is going to try to come early, too. She's anxious to meet Henri, since he seems to be the talk of the place." Nikki was facing her mom but moved her eyes to see Henri's reaction. He was amused.

Roxy came in and heard the laughter from their table. She focused in on Henri and liked what she saw. He was one handsome dude, that's for sure!

Roxy went right up to Henri. "So you are the Frenchman who has taken over the inn like a whirlwind. There are a lot of people staying here, but to my knowledge, you are the only one I keep hearing about." Henri stood up and kissed her extended hand, guessing that Roxy might expect that from him. He was right.

"And I have heard favorable things about you, Mademoiselle Roxy." He held out her chair while she sat down, eating up all the attention she was receiving.

"You are a lyric writer, that is right?"

"I am working hard at becoming a good one. So far, Ted and I have been lucky. Our album went over much better than we had ever dreamed possible. Now we're really challenging ourselves by attempting to put music to the wonderful book that Eric wrote." As soon as the words were out of her mouth, she regretted mentioning Eric and, perhaps causing some jealous feelings in Henri. She was put at ease by his kind words.

"I must buy this book and I will picture how you will make it into a musical. That must be very difficult."

"We've already made a good start and it helps that we're able to use some of the songs from our album. Although we haven't a deadline, we're trying to move it along so that John can fit us into his heavy schedule at the music hall."

Nikki spoke up. "Henri, Ted and Roxy are two of the most talented people that I have ever worked with. I should say, that I have ever met, since I haven't worked with many people."

They all laughed. Roxy countered with, "I have a feeling that in time you'll work with many musicians."

Ted came in and stopped at their table. "Now this looks like a cozy, little group. May I join you?"

They chatted on for about fifteen minutes and the lounge began to fill up. John waved at them from behind the bar and a few more waitresses came in to help out. When their waitress came to the table, Henri said, "Ah, Marie. How nice to see you again. Is little Mary feeling better tonight?"

Eileen almost fell off her seat. *How does he do that?* She wondered.

"My friends, this is Marie and she had to go home today to see how her little girl was doing. She had been feeling ill." He looked at Marie again. "It is hard to be a working mother, yes?"

His sincere concern lit up Marie's face. "I do my best, Henri."

Ted and Nikki didn't order and went to the piano instead. Eric was in the doorway and made his way to their table. Henri stood and extended his hand.

"And you are Eric, yes?"

Eric returned his firm handshake and said, "Yes, I am. Nice to meet you, Henri. I hear that you are new to our neck of the woods."

"Yes, and it has won me over. No wonder it is so popular with the tourists."

Ted played a soft introduction and Nikki took the mike. The room grew quiet.

She wanted to address the diverse crowd in the room. "I have been told that we have a lot of seniors here tonight, so I would like to sing a few songs just for you and hope to bring back some pleasant memories. The first one was made famous by Elvis Presley back in 1956. You might not be aware of the fact that when it was originally written by George Poulton in 1861 it was called 'Aura Lee.' Yes, I am talking about the very beautiful, 'Love Me Tender.' I hope you enjoy it."

Then Nikki sang her own version making it even more tender than the name implied. Henri wasn't expecting such perfection from her and when she was finished, he clapped the loudest and longest of the appreciative patrons.

"My next oldie will most likely have you remembering the famous Andrews Sisters. 'I Can Dream, Can't I?' is the romantic number I'd like to sing next." Again she held everyone's attention and received a big hand.

John had worked his way over to the stage and took the mike from Nikki. John knew Henri only as Eileen's client. He hadn't heard of any romantic interests, so it came as a surprise to those at the table that he singled Henri out in front of Eric.

"Folks, I would like to say that we are honored to have a famous Parisian interior designer here with us. As a matter of fact, if you're a regular customer here, you probably noticed a few changes in this room, like new plants here and there, and other decorations done at the suggestion of Henri Broleau visiting from Paris, France." John signaled for Henri to stand as people were clapping. Embarrassed, Henri half stood and then quickly sat down. Eileen felt so bad for Eric that she couldn't join in the recognition and instead looked sadly as Eric politely clapped for Henri.

John turned the mike over to Nikki and she announced, "I would like to sing a song that was not only well known in France, but also in the States. 'Lilli Marlene' was made famous by Marlene Dietrich during wartime." As she sang, she looked directly at Henri and walked with the mike to sing in front of him. She knew that he would know the words to this French song so she signaled for him to join in. To her complete surprise, Henri harmonized in a great baritone voice to the delight of the audience. Eileen wished she had never suggested that Eric join them.

Then from somewhere in the room, someone yelled, "Encore" and Nikki pulled Henri to the stage to repeat singing "Lilli Marlene." At any other time, Henri would have been happy to join her, but just knowing how Eric must be feeling made him regret the encore. John was the only one of the gang who was thrilled by what had happened. Had he known the situation, he would have understood the somber faces on his friends.

At intermission, Nikki went straight to the bar and took John aside and explained the awkward moment that he had caused. No one realized that John hadn't heard, so there was no blame, but John still felt a deep hurt for his friend Eric.

These friends hadn't realized that Henri spent a good part his life dealing with all kinds of people and unforeseen situations. There was no way he was going to allow Eric to remain uncomfortable. Henri started relating a whole new set of stories about his odd bunch of customers that he had to please by decorating their houses and apartments. It didn't take long before, as usual, he had everyone, including Eric, roaring with laughter. The intermission extended a little longer than usual as Ted and Nikki didn't want to miss what Henri was saying.

Once back onstage Nikki sought to please the younger clientele in the audience and announced a Carrie Underwood song, "All American Girl," followed by Michael Bublé's "Everything." Nikki tried to delight all her fans, and knowing this, they returned again and again. This time she had a new fan in Henri.

At the end of the performance, they all sat at the table enjoying more light-hearted tales. Henri went out of his way to include Eric in the conversation. When Eric said he had been to Paris, Henri asked for a detailed description of every place he had visited. It gave Eric a chance to shine as he described the history of the art work he had seen at the Louvre. He talked about the artists and their particular styles. It was obvious that he was a highly intelligent man. Eileen was so proud of him and also of Henri for giving Eric his moment. All in all, it was a very successful evening, even though Eileen was still confused about her deepest feelings for these two men in her life.

Eileen spent a restless night. Yet she still woke at her usual early hour and felt the need to keep her regular routine. She hoped that Eric wouldn't be there to add to her confusion.

Arriving at the beach, she saw Eric's bike. Then she spotted Eric sitting at their bench writing in his notebook. He looked up but didn't hold out his arms in greeting.

"Good morning, Eileen. I suppose it's too soon for you to have sorted out your dilemma?" He saw her troubled look and continued on, "It's okay. You don't have to answer if you aren't ready. If you need more time, I must say that I can understand after meeting Henri. He's delightful company and he has a magnetic personality. If he were fly paper, he'd be full of flies." Eileen managed a weak smile. Eric said, "Just a poor attempt to make light of a serious situation."

Eileen didn't reply but she sat next to him and removed her sneakers. He was watching her in silence.

"Look, Eileen, I'll just sit here and write while you take your walk. I'm not going to impose myself on you. It's obvious to me that you need time to be alone. As long as I know that I am still in the race, I can be patient."

Eric noticed that she was wearing a darker pair of sunglasses than usual and he wondered if it was to conceal her eyes. How he wished he could help her.

"Thanks for being so understanding, Eric. You're right. I really must walk alone this morning."

He sadly watched her go off alone. He decided that there was no way that he could continue writing, for he couldn't take his eyes off her. The questions were painful. *Would he ever walk beside her again? God, how could he live without her if she decided to be with Henri?* The thoughts were so troubling that he had to leave.

He could barely see Eileen walking in the distance. Was that symbolic? Would she continue to walk out of his life? He got up and glanced down at her pink sneakers and lovingly touched them before he left.

As Eileen came closer to their bench, she realized Eric was no longer there. She longed to see him and to let him know how much he was loved. What had she done to this dear man? How many men would stand by her under these circumstances? Her mind, like his, was full of questions.

She put on her sneakers and vowed to work on his painting this afternoon. She had set it aside to fill Henri's orders. Well, Henri could wait!

Chapter 11

Once home, Eileen took out the painting and studied it. She wanted to use a limited palette. She felt that repeating colors coordinated the whole composition. Thus, the same pink of the sneakers was carefully incorporated into the beach sand around them. The legs and seat of the bench from the side formed a frame giving predominance to the sneakers. She felt she was painting a part of herself and preserving it for Eric's memories of their shared lives. But would it be representing the past or the future?

Eileen needed a break to free her mind. She made a light lunch and lingered over her tea. Then the phone rang. It was Henri.

"I am taking your advice, Eileen, and calling you first. Have you completed any more sketches for my approval?"

"No, Henri, I had another commission that I need to complete. I may not have time to work on your assignment today. Sorry!"

"Not to worry, Eileen. I'd like to sample another restaurant tonight. Is there one around here that has a nice band to serenade us?"

"Us, Henri?"

"Yes, us! I know that a good hostess would never let a visiting client go off without an escort, so where would you suggest that we dine?"

"Did anyone ever tell you that you are pushy?"

"Pushy? That is a funny word, Eileen. I like to think that I am inviting a very pretty lady to accompany me for a pleasant evening."

"Okay, Henri, you win! Yes, there is a restaurant that has good food and a small band, but it's a distance from here. Do you wish to drive twenty-five miles for such a restaurant?"

"I am always willing to go a ways to have what I want, Eileen. You should know that!"

There was a pause and then she answered. "You're right. I do know that about you, Henri."

"I will pick you up at 5:30. Is that a good time for you, ma chérie?"

"I will be ready for you." And then she hung up.

Eileen watched for his car and stepped out when he pulled in. She wore a smartly-styled deep brown suit. Her silk blouse had a pattern that picked up the deep brown with a complementary rose and a pale yellow. Her hair was loose and softly curled. Brown spike-heeled shoes and a brown handbag completed the ensemble. Henri came out of the car and opened the car door for her while admiring her attractive outfit.

"You will have to give me directions because I didn't look it up before leaving. Not that I would mind getting lost if I were with you."

He gave her a side glance that showed he liked that idea.

"Have you bought your return ticket to France yet, Henri?"

"In truth, I have been holding off to see just where I stand with you, Eileen. Why? You aren't anxious to get rid of me, are you?"

"I am thoroughly enjoying being with you, but I am trying to get a time frame for completing your order. For some of the photos, my ideas flow nicely onto the sketch pad the first time. For others, I keep changing where I place things and, in general, rearranging whole compositions. I want to make certain that we agree on all this before I start the actual paintings."

"That is understandable. I can't imagine my not liking what you have designed."

As they drove along, Eileen noted each point of interest and related a little history that went with it. Henri liked to learn the background and she was a good teacher. It made the ride pass quickly and they soon drove up to a large wooden structure with many picture windows and a welcoming front porch. The cars in the parking lot were all expensive, so Henri's rented car, a new Porsche, fit in just fine.

Although the dining room was large to allow for a very small dancing area and a section for the band, it still maintained a cozy atmosphere in the setup of the tables and use of many plants and soft lighting. They were seated at a spot that allowed for privacy with the use of dividers and more plants. It suited them just fine.

Eileen excused herself and went to the ladies' room. When she came back, Henri was gone. The waiter quickly came up to her and said that Henri had been talking with the other waiter about choosing a good wine. When he was told about the wine cellar, Henri had asked to see it for himself. He left the message that Eileen was not to worry, because he would be right back after he had picked out a suitable selection.

Eileen wondered if the restaurant had ever encountered anyone like Henri before. Then she looked up to see him coming with the waiter, chatting away about good years for wine.

With his arm around the waiter's shoulder, Henri said, "Eileen, this is Robert and he agrees that you must sample this vintage wine." Robert placed two glasses on the table and poured the wine.

"To a lovely lady. May I always share my wine with her."

Eileen shook her head, ignoring what he had just implied.

The wine was delicious and they sipped it while Henri studied the menu. Robert suggested more than one selection and then Henri looked at Eileen and said, "Why don't we let Robert surprise us? Would that be all right with you?" And, of course, Eileen agreed.

Robert was beaming. Such confidence in his taste was rare indeed. "You won't be disappointed, I promise." Then he left to talk personally with the chef.

"That was nice of you, Henri. You certainly made his day."

"It was obvious to me that he really knew about all the dishes that the chef prepared, so I wasn't exactly taking a chance. Robert hasn't the easiest of jobs, and I felt he could use a little recognition for his know-how.

"Well, chérie, I will soon have to go back to France, and I want you to come with me. We could share my apartment, or I could buy a house for us. I am hoping that you will agree to live with me. Paris is a wonderful place for you to promote your work and move your paintings. If, after six months or so you feel that our relationship isn't for you, you could move back here to Maine. Won't you give it a try, Eileen?"

"You are asking me to give up my life here -- my daughter, my business in New York, and my friends and studio here in Maine. I don't think I could do that, Henri, even for you." She was looking him straight in the eye and saw his deep disappointment. He tried to think of a solution.

"For me to move here and live with you would mean I would continually have to fly back and forth to Europe, where my work is known and sought after by a steady clientele. Even if I agreed on such an arrangement, I would have to be gone for very long periods of time to supervise the workmanship in carrying out my designs."

After a silent pause, he added, "I think the fates have conspired against us, Eileen. Either way, the sacrifices would be a constant strain on us, yes?"

Sadly, Eileen agreed.

Robert arrived with escargots in garlic butter to start the meal.

"Ah, a nice French surprise, uh, Robert? We shall see if it tastes as good as it looks."

Robert didn't move while he waited for Henri to taste the escargots and give his verdict.

Henri shut his eyes as if to further concentrate on the taste.

"C'est magnifique, Robert!" Robert nodded in pleasure and left them to enjoy eating the rest of the escargots.

After a while, they saw Robert returning with another dish.

"What have we here, Robert?" Henri asked.

"Tournedos with Béarnaise sauce, another French specialty."

Henri smiled and said, "I have prepared this dish for friends with success. I will see if we have similar recipes."

Robert watched anxiously. Then Henri remarked, "Again, your chef has outdone himself. Eileen, don't you agree?"

Eileen did agree and asked how Henri made his dish. She hadn't expected his lengthy reply.

"First, I make the Béarnaise sauce by combining vinegar, wine, tarragon, and finely chopped shallot. You have to bring it to a boil and then simmer it for ten minutes. Then it involves straining the mixture and cooking over a double boiler. With a wire whisk, you beat in egg yolks. And later on, you have to add butter. You broil the beef for five minutes, and turn it, coating it with butter and then finish broiling it. Once you arrange the beef on a plate, you add the sauce and, voilà, you have your dish."

Eileen looked impressed. "Henri, you are a man of many talents."

"I am a man with many friends whom I enjoy entertaining and I am, also, asked out a lot. This would be a part of your life, too, Eileen, if you would so choose."

"I am sure that you are never lonely, Henri. You like people too much to let that happen."

While they were talking, Robert continued to place tempting dishes in front of them. There were tomatoes Provençale, *petits pois*, and potatoes au gratin. He also brought in a basket of hot scones to sample.

Eileen didn't think she could possibly eat any more, but she knew that Robert didn't think the meal complete without dessert. She said the only thing that she might be able to eat would be some fruit. And so Robert was back in no time with a *tarte tatin*, an upside-down apple tart with whipped cream. It would be wonderful to eat when hungry, but she could only manage a few delicious bites.

Henri slowly managed to finish his dessert. "I must go to the kitchen and compliment your chef, Robert. And you, my friend, have pleased me very much with your selections."

Henri excused himself and went off as Robert brought Eileen a fresh cup of coffee.

It wasn't long before Henri was back with the chef himself. He introduced Eileen to Leonard and proceeded to tell her all about where the man had worked before and how he had learned to prepare French dishes in Canada. After Leonard left, they drank their coffee and watched the small band set up and start to play softly while people dined. The next thing Eileen knew Henri stood up and took her hand.

"Come, Eileen, and we will dance."

"But, Henri, there is no one dancing. It's just background music."

"Music is music and it is a chance to hold you in my arms." With that, he led her to the small dance floor. The musicians were watching and seemed pleased that their music was being appreciated. They increased the volume just a little as they played some favorite old love songs especially for the dancing couple.

Eileen had no trouble following his lead. He was a great dancer, which should not have surprised her. He held her close and managed to kiss her cheek more than once. She noticed that he had on an aftershave lotion that made his closeness even more desirable. He sang softly near her ear and she felt herself falling under his spell. His scent, the music, his singing, his closeness were all combining with the glow that the rich wine had cast. The musicians were convinced that they were serenading a couple deeply in love. Right now, Eileen might have agreed with them.

"Eileen, you fit in my arms like they were meant just for you. This is where you belong, you know?"

"You are making it very difficult for me to think rationally, Henri."

"Good. Think irrationally all you want to as long as you stay with me." This was all too much for Eileen to handle.

"I think I want to sit down now, Henri."

He walked her back to her seat and excused himself. She watched him go over and talk with the musicians. Before she knew, it they had stopped playing and were listening to him intently. "Now, what?" she thought. Next thing she knew they were laughing as he walked back to her.

"I had to thank them for playing such romantic music for us. I told them about a band in Paris that played that song with a different ending and I hummed it for them. They liked it and they are going to try using it next time they play it."

"Henri, do you mind if I ask you a personal question?" She looked serious.

"I would never mind anything you asked, I am sure."

"I was just wondering, when you were married, did you slow down at all?"

"No, I guess that was part of the problem. I had too many friends in my life and my wife wanted to be alone with me more often. She remarried and has started a family. We are still good friends. Does that answer your question, Eileen?"

"Yes. It was the answer that I expected."

Eileen couldn't have asked for a better evening. She had to admit, Henri certainly knew how to wine and dine a lady.

On the ride home, he talked about places in Paris that he wanted to show her. The pictures he cleverly painted in her mind promoted a deep desire in her to return to Paris and see it through Henri's eyes. After listening to him, she realized there was no way that he would ever leave his beloved city.

When they finally arrived at her house, Henri hopped out of the car to open the door for her, making it difficult for her not to invite him inside. Eileen reluctantly did ask if he wanted to see her last sketch or if he would rather wait until tomorrow.

Henri had a knack for reading people's minds and Eileen was no exception, and so he answered for her.

"I see that you are tired, Eileen, and that you still have a lot on your mind. You know that I would like to extend our evening together but I respect your wishes. Should we say good night, Eileen?"

At this point, she was totally confused. Part of her wanted to invite him in, knowing he would want more from her; and then what would she do? Not wanting to face that dilemma, she said, "Henri, if you don't mind, I'd like to thank you for a wonderful evening and say good night here."

He held her face in his hands.

"Well, I would not be telling the truth if I said I didn't mind, but I am happy about the time we did spend together."

He took her in his arms and kissed her gently at first, and then more passionately as his embrace forced her body tighter against him. He stirred strong emotions in her, causing her to feel lightheaded and her knees to weaken almost to the point of being unsupportive. To break the spell, she lowered her arms from behind his neck and braced her hands on his arms to unlock their close embrace.

Steadying her breathing, she managed to say, "Please, Henri, let us say goodbye now before this goes any further!"

Reluctantly, he released her. "Whatever you say, Eileen, but you did return my kiss, no?"

"Yes, I did. You are a hard man to resist. Please try to understand, Henri, that you do mean a lot to me. I hope you know that?"

Seemingly resigned to the change in his plans, he said, "For now, it is enough. I will see you tomorrow and perhaps you will have some good news for me." As he started to walk to his car, he stopped and turned for one more look at Eileen standing on her porch.

"Sweet dreams, and may I be a part of them."

Eileen smiled and only said, "Good night, Henri."

The last thing Eileen wanted was to lead him on. It seemed that she had managed to hurt two very dear men. She went inside and in her bedroom picked up Dan's photo, which she kept on her dresser.

"Oh, Dan, I wish that you could choose for me. I feel so drained and incapable of making any sensible decisions. You and I, Dan, had such a good marriage that maybe it has made me too anxious to go that route again." She placed his photo back on her dresser and prepared for bed.

Chapter 12

Ted and Roxy were almost finished with the musical score based on Eric's story. They had worked diligently on it and, for the most part, they were satisfied. After two straight hours of work, Roxy told Ted that they needed a break. She suggested a visit to the beach.

"Perhaps the fresh air will clear our heads and inspire us, or should I say inspire me? The problem is not with your great music, Ted. It is just that I get these writer's block moments that throw me."

Once at the beach, they headed to Eric and Eileen's bench. Ted stretched out his long legs, leaned back and rested his arms on the back of the bench. He looked and felt contented. Roxy was still in her work mode. There was a gentle shore breeze, which they both found refreshing. Roxy had brought along a small tape recorder which had Ted's compositions on it for Roxy to work with when she wasn't with him at the piano.

"I am having the most trouble with the leading man's sad song when he is convinced that he has lost his love. It isn't good enough or emotional enough each time I rewrite the lyrics. I try to put myself in his place, but it just isn't working."

Ted didn't seem the least bit worried about it, but he offered her a suggestion.

"Roxy, why don't you picture Eric and his thoughts now that he thinks he may lose Eileen? To be truthful, Rox, I wish that she wouldn't put him through this guessing game!" Ted sat upright now with a concerned look on his face. "Didn't your heart ache for him last Saturday night? Much as I enjoyed Henri, I thought it was unfair to have Eric sitting there like a lost soul. God, before Henri came into the picture, you couldn't have met a happier guy! Yeah, Rox, think of Eric."

Roxy nodded in agreement, and said, "You know, Ted, you're right! I'll do that for a true perspective of a lost love. Actually, when he is the professor in class, he covers his emotions so well that I forget about his private life."

Silence followed while they reflected on their discussion. Then Roxy said, "I'd love to get him to talk about his feelings and help me express the sadness more accurately." She looked at Ted tenderly. "It was different when I thought that I had lost your love. That was sheer panic on my part. With Eric, he was already in a serious relationship. What a blow to his ego, not to mention his dreams!"

"Don't be too hard on Eileen, Rox. After meeting that Frenchman I could understand anyone going off with him, couldn't you?"

Roxy readily agreed that Henri is a first-class charmer, but she couldn't picture him settling down to married life.

They relaxed for a while in silence then Roxy spoke up.

"I have your music on my tape, Ted, so I plan to keep listening to it in my room tonight. I'll keep Eric in mind and that way I feel certain that the right words will come to express such sadness."

They watched the gulls and walked the shore before leaving the beach. They were comfortable together and right now, that is what mattered the most.

True to her word, that night Roxy played the tape, and this time the sadness in Ted's composition moved her to create the most touching lyrics she had ever written. She knew that after class tomorrow, Eric would have to hear it to critique it just as he did each of the other songs. It bothered her to do this to him but, after all, it was his book, so he had to expect such lyrics would be written. She went to bed with a heavy heart.

The next morning after Poetry class, Roxy remained in her seat. Eric waited until the room emptied out before going to her.

"You look a bit troubled, Rox! Is there something I can straighten out for you?"

"Oh, it's just another sheet of my lyrics for your approval, Professor. I've finished the leading man's lost love song." When she saw his sad expression, she said, "If you would rather wait a few days before doing this, it's okay."

Eric understood the underlining meaning in her question.

"No, that won't be necessary." Then he noticed her tape recorder. "Looks like I am in luck! I'll get to hear Ted's music, too. I've been so pleased with his work so far."

Roxy asked if he wanted to read her lyrics while the music was on or if he wanted her to sing them with the music to see how they fit. Her voice wouldn't do it justice, she said, but maybe it would make a clearer picture. At Eric's request, Roxy ended up singing her touching words to Ted's haunting love song.

Eric hadn't expected it to hit home like it did. He found it necessary to turn his head in order to compose himself. It was almost as though Roxy had written it for him. When she finally finished, he turned towards her with his eyes brimming with tears that he tried to hide. "Roxy, what you wrote is absolutely beautiful! There is nothing I would change this time. Now, if you will excuse me, I have to stop at the library."

He turned and left Roxy. Since she valued his opinion, she was pleased that he liked it, yet troubled that she had subjected the professor to a resurfacing of his deep hurt.

She returned to her dorm to wait for Ted's arrival. She was thankful that she had enough energy to keep up her studies and still spend time with Ted. She was excited because Ted was coming to pick her up and take her out to dinner.

She was deep in thought when there was a knock on her door. A shudder went through her when she opened the door and saw Tex standing there with a foolish grin on his face.

"Boy, are you in luck, Rox! There's a motorcycle meet this weekend and I am taking you."

"No, you are not taking me, Tex. Now, please leave."

He pushed his way inside and grabbed her arm in a tight grip.

"I wasn't planning on getting rough, but if you force me, we can do it that way, too."

"Have you lost your mind?" At this point, she knew she had to be careful.

"You used to love those meets, Rox. Once you're on your way, it'll all come back to you and you'll be thrilled to be with your Tex." He pulled out a pamphlet which advertised the meet.

"Take a look at this, Rox! Remember how great it was."

"Get out, now! If you don't leave, I will scream and there are others on this floor who will hear me."

An ugly expression appeared on his face as he reached in his pocket and pulled out his jack knife.

"You don't really want my initials carved on your pretty arm, do you?"

Roxy knew anything was possible when it came to his threats.

"Just pack your things and leave with me and you'll be just fine."

Roxy's mind was racing. She felt she could better plan her escape if she went along with him and waited until he calmed down.

Still pointing his knife at her, he sat on the bed and watched her. Wordlessly, she did as she was told. He tossed the pamphlet on the night stand, and said, "That's a good girl!"

Roxy zipped up her backpack and announced, "I've got to use the john first." She shut the door of the bathroom, grabbed the soap and wrote on the mirror: "Help. Tex forced me out." She flushed the toilet and hurried out. Then they left.

"We're takin' your car, Babe. My buddy dropped me off here and now we need to meet him at the meet. He has my bike in his truck just waiting for you and me. You'll be doing the driving and I'll be givin' the instructions. Once you relax, I know you're going to love it just like you used to."

Not long after they had left, Ted arrived at the dorm. The first thing he noticed was Roxy's car was missing. Puzzled, he hurried up to her room and found it unlocked, which added to his concern. He called her name and checked the closet to find some of her clothes missing. Next, he went into the bathroom and the first thing he saw was the message on the mirror. His heart sank. He tried her cell phone number, but there was no answer. He then phoned the police and described her red Mercedes-Benz and the only part of her license plate number he remembered. It was enough to start an all-out search.

If only Ted had some idea as to where Tex was headed, it would be a big help. He tried to reach her on the phone once more, but again there was no answer. He felt so helpless. Maybe there was some clue in the room, he thought. He spotted a paper on the bed stand and read it. It described the motor meet to be held this weekend.

"That's it! That must be where he is taking her." He phoned the police again with this new information and then headed out himself.

The closest police station had received the description, so all along the route the police were alerted to look for her car.

Roxy's hands were sweating as she tightly gripped the steering wheel. Her mind was going a mile a minute trying to figure out her next move. It was a long shot, but she finally knew what she would do.

"Ya know, Tex, you're right! I remember the fun we had at those meets. Maybe we can hook up with some of our old friends, you think?"

Tex wasn't the brightest guy, so he began to relax.

"I knew it! Now, you're talkin'."

They traveled on in silence as Roxy thought back to her dorm and the message on the mirror. She knew that Ted would look in the bathroom, but how long ago was that?

Roxy always used to drive fast. Now, she was deliberately speeding. They were passing cars and laughing. Twenty minutes down the road, she heard the siren and saw the flashing lights in her rearview mirror. She pulled over.

The officer came over and ordered them to step outside.

Tex was incensed. "What for? Speeding?"

Roxy showed her driver's license and immediately the officer knew he had the right car.

He told Tex to put his hands behind his back and he was handcuffed. Tex was fuming.

"Hey, what is this?"

"You are under arrest for kidnapping, so get in the cruiser now."

After she made a statement to the police, Roxy was able to text Ted and drive back to the dorm. A relieved Ted was waiting for her when she arrived.

Jack and Anne were at their beach home. Jack needed to check on the music hall and the progress Ted and Roxy were making on the songs. He had no doubt that he'd made the right move in hiring John to put it all together. So far, he'd done an excellent job. When he learned that Ted and Roxy had finished the musical score, he was surprised. He was aware that they'd been laboring many extra hours over it, but it still amazed him that they'd actually completed the work in such a short time.

Jack met with them and arranged a preview for his approval. He invited John, Eric, and Eileen to join them. Because Nikki had been listening to the musical score as they'd composed it, and was familiar with the words and music, Jack asked if she could sing the whole musical for them. He was pleased when she accepted.

"I'll have to read the whole thing as I sing for you, but you can get a good idea of where all this is going. You'll just have to visualize the male parts unless you want to have Ted try to do them."

The preview performance was held at an informal gathering at Jack's house. Eric couldn't back out. This musical was based on his novel and he wanted to see and hear what these two talented people did with it. He knew Eileen would be invited, too, but hoped that no one had decided to include Henri.

Eric arrived early and looked over the sheet music Ted had composed with Roxy. All the pieces of the puzzle were coming together. He heard Eileen's voice and knew that she had arrived. He wondered if she would sit next to him or if she would feel more comfortable with a separation between them. As soon as he saw her, all the strong feelings that he felt for her surfaced. She smiled and came over and sat down next to him.

"This must be an exciting moment for you, Eric. And to think that it all started with your casual writing at the beach! I can't wait to hear it."

Eileen put him at ease and Ted began a brief piano introduction. Nikki had to read as she sang, but her beautiful voice impressed all of them. Ted sang the male parts with a passable voice which was, at least, right on key. Even so, he moved them all to tears when he sang the "lost love" song that Roxy had worked so hard on. Eric couldn't look at Eileen during the song or he knew he would have to excuse himself. Eileen could sense his emotions and she tried to cover her own without much luck. At the end, when the lovers are once again united, the music soared to express their great joy.

When the whole concert was over the little audience applauded loudly. John rushed over to Ted and Roxy and couldn't contain his elation.

"I can't believe you two actually wrote this! It's wonderful! Now, all we need is the script and it will be ready for the public. I've spoken to the conductor of our orchestra that has been playing for the musicals we've produced here. He wants to work with you, Ted, to write the arrangements for each instrument." Ted nodded.

John looked at Nikki and said, "I know that you're very busy, but I was wondering if you could give some thought to the scenery? It doesn't have to be too elaborate, just passable. The same goes for costumes."

"I already have some ideas that I will run by you when I make some sketches." Nikki always came through for them and they were appreciative.

All and all it had been a very successful afternoon.

Eileen hadn't been home very long after the concert when the phone rang. It was Henri.

"Is it alright if I come over to see what you have come up with for the paintings?"

"Yes, they are all ready for you." She didn't feel like having any company, least of all someone that played with her emotions, but she did want to get this out of the way.

Henri arrived anxious to see Eileen once again. He skipped a few steps as he made his way up to the porch. As Eileen opened the door she was, once again, aware of the old attraction coming on strong. He lightly kissed her in greeting. She had laid all the sketches out on the table and one by one they discussed her ideas for the finished paintings. Henry suggested a few color changes and asked for rearrangements of some compositions. They also agreed on a different size for one. When they finished, Eileen put on some coffee for them and took out some muffins she had made in the morning.

"You've put a lot of work into all this and it shows. When do you expect to start on the actual paintings?"

"I'll start tomorrow, Henri. I can't give you a time frame, but since I know what I am to do for each one, it shouldn't take too long." He was watching her so intently that it made her uncomfortable.

"And have you thought about what you want to do in your personal life?"

"Thought about it, yes. Come to any positive conclusions, no."

Henri looked disappointed. "You do realize that I must get back to Paris soon? I was so hoping that you would be at my side." Eileen looked down at the table because she couldn't bear to meet his eyes. Henri continued.

"Eileen, we would have a wonderful life together. It would be my goal to make you happy. There is so much to see and do. Not only that, but the interesting people that I would introduce you to, people in the art world that you would have a lot in common with and could share ideas with. I promise you would never be bored."

"When would you say you must leave, Henri?"

"I had planned on leaving in another week. Surely, you would have an answer in a day or two so that you could make arrangements to leave with me!" When she didn't answer, he went on, "With Nikki living here she can send you whatever you need. Everything in your studio can be shipped or I can duplicate your art supplies at my studio. It really isn't as complicated as you might imagine. As the kids like to say, no big deal!"

"You see, Henri, that is where you're wrong! It is a very big deal to me." She stood up and held on to the back of her chair for support. "I can't deny that I like being with you. And I have no doubt that you are a fantastic lover, but I need stability and commitment. Call me old-fashioned if you like, but these are things that are very important to me. To leave everything and move in with you, no matter how great we are together, is asking too much of me." Without realizing it, she was arriving at a decision and Henri's troubled look showed that he knew it, too.

"Can you see my point of view, Henri?"

Henri had stood up and was in front of her. He put his arms around her and hugged her while he whispered in her ear. "How can I give you up, Eileen? Is there anything I can do to change your mind?" Their faces were inches apart and her resolve was dissolving. He kissed her with all the passion that he was feeling and both were breathing faster.

"We have spent so little time together, Eileen. Would you consider going to Paris for a trial run? I know I have enough love in my heart to convince you that this will work."

Eileen's head was spinning. She was tempted to accept his plan when she was in his arms.

"Henri, I don't function well when pressured and I am feeling pressured now. I am not trying to lead you on, Henri, but this is too serious not to give it ample time for examining all aspects of such a big move. Please try to understand. If you must have an answer right now, then I will have to say no."

Henri pulled away and shook his head. "You leave me no choice, Eileen. I have to wait with the hope that you will decide to accept my offer." He had his hand on the doorknob. "I can tell you this, Eileen, if you do go with me, I promise you will never regret it. I will personally see to that. Goodnight, Eileen." He left her standing there with tears in her eyes and more confused than ever.

Later Nikki arrived home and guessed that something had transpired that bothered her mother.

"Okay, Mom, what happened while I was gone?"

"Sometimes I wonder if you really do read minds, Nikki."

"Well, I can see the two coffee cups at the sink so I am guessing that one of the men in your life visited you. Am I right?"

"Henri was here to see the plans for his paintings. He pressed me for an answer about going to Paris to live with him. He even suggested a trial period before making a full commitment."

"Now, let me get this straight. He is asking you to move in with him for the rest of your life, but there was no mention of marriage? Right?"

"Well, now that you mention it, that's right."

"How convenient for him. He will give up nothing. He will continue his life in the same house and work in the same studio while keeping the same friends in the same country. Yet he expects you to give up your life as you now live it. Leave your daughter, house, friends, job, and country to live with him. Who stands the most to lose, Mom?"

"I guess that I had already arrived at that conclusion on his deal, Nikki. You had put it correctly once before when you said that you would pick Henri to go with to a party and Eric to spend the rest of your life with."

Eileen looked relieved and said to Nikki, "As usual, you have helped me sort this out with your level-headed thinking. I can always count on you guiding me in the right direction." Eileen kissed her daughter. "Thanks, honey."

"You're welcome. Now, what have you planned for supper?"

Over dinner, Eileen told Nikki that she would let Eric know that Henri was like a whirlwind that swept her off her feet, but that nothing happened between them except the sheer fun of enjoying each other's company. She could only imagine what had been going through Eric's mind since Henri had arrived. Eileen hadn't gone to the beach in days and wondered if Eric had continued to go. At any rate, she would know in the morning because she planned on resuming her beach walks.

The next morning was a nice sunny day. Eileen wore a light blue hooded jacket over a white T-shirt. Her navy shorts had a pink trim which matched her sneakers. The bench was empty, so she assumed that Eric hadn't been coming as he used to. She placed her sneakers in their usual spot and went for her walk.

Eric arrived and did a double take when he saw Eileen's car. He didn't want to build up his hopes too high but felt maybe she had made a decision. The empty spot beside their bench had saddened him, but now as he approached the bench the pink sneakers came into view. Eric spotted Eileen in the far distance about to make her way back and decided to just sit and watch her coming towards him.

When Eileen reached him, she seemed happy he was there.

"Good morning, Eric. I missed our times at the beach. You've been very patient with me and I appreciate that." She sat next to him and her nearness made him eager to hear her answer.

"Eileen, please tell me you have made your decision. This waiting is disrupting my whole life."

"No more waiting, Eric. Henri is leaving shortly and I am remaining here with you."

He could no longer hold in his emotions and he threw his arms around her and said, "Thank God, Eileen. I really thought I had lost you. I just couldn't figure out how to compete with someone like Henri."

"Henri will have no trouble finding someone to take my place. He has a lot going for him, but let's not talk about Henri, okay?"

"Fine by me."

"I think that our friends will be pleased to hear that I'm staying and that we'll be back together." Eric couldn't stop smiling and he kept his arm around her as they walked to the parking lot and headed for the inn.

Jack, in the meanwhile, had met with John to discuss the plans for the musical.

"Now that the music scores are ready, we need to have the script in place. Since it's based on Eric's book, I feel he's the best one to draft the speaking parts for the actors. I plan on asking him if he'll take on the job. Are you in agreement with that?"

John looked surprised. "I took it for granted that Eric would be doing it."

"Good. Next I feel that we should start auditioning for the singers so that they can start studying the music." Jack looked serious and said, "I just can't get it out of my mind that Nikki is our best choice for the leading lady. Her voice is perfect for the part and I have a feeling that she can act as well. If you want, we could skip auditioning for that role and just ask her if she would accept the part. Should she have her doubts, well, then we could audition for someone else. What are your thoughts about this?"

John smiled. "After hearing her at your house, I can't imagine anyone else in the role. I hope that you ask her soon so we'll all know her answer."

"That I will, my friend." He turned and left John feeling pleased with how things were shaping up.

When Jack arrived at the inn to look for Nikki, he saw his friends gathered around Eric and Eileen.

"What's all the excitement?"

He guessed that Eileen had made her decision.

After the conversation died down, Eileen needed to find Henri and let him know that she wouldn't be accompanying him on his trip to Paris. It was news that she dreaded telling him but she also knew that he had to be told by her and not someone at the inn. After checking at the desk, they rang his room. When he answered the call, he was asked if Eileen could go up to his room.

"By all means, send her up please."

Henri was waiting at the door when she arrived and he suspected the worse.

"So you have decided to stay here, yes?"

Eileen nodded.

"*C'est dommage*, Eileen. I was so hopeful." He took both her hands in his and looked into her eyes.

"Ah, ma chérie, do not feel sorry for me. I want you to be happy with your decision, but if you should ever feel that you made a mistake, just pack your bags and come to me." He put his hand under her chin and raised her head so that she would look at him.

"You promise?"

With a sad smile Eileen said, "I promise, Henri."

"I will be leaving tomorrow and you can ship the pictures when they are done. I am sure that they will meet with my customer's approval." Instead of inviting her to stay awhile, he said "If you will excuse me, I have some packing to do and some phone calls to place." As she turned to leave, she heard him say, "Tell Eric that he is a very lucky guy. *Á bientôt*, Eileen."

"*Au revoir*, Henri." When he closed the door there was something very final about it.

Nikki was in the dining room with a cup of coffee and her notebook. She was sitting at a corner table planning her marketing designs when she heard her name being paged. Arriving at the desk, she was surprised to see that Jack had paged her.

"Nikki, let's go back to your table. I have a proposition to make to you and we can talk there." He signaled for another coffee and sat down with her.

"I'll get right to the point. We need to advertise for auditions for the singing roles."

Nikki agreed that she would get right on it.

"John and I both would like you to accept the female lead. Are you interested?"

She hadn't known that they were even considering her for that role. "Jack, I have never acted. You do realize that?"

"I really don't think that will be a problem, Nikki."

Thrilled at the idea she said, "I am flattered that you both have so much confidence in me. I know I could handle the singing, but I will have to work with a good director to know what's expected of me."

Jack was used to his persuasive powers so he wasn't all that surprised by her acceptance. "We were hoping that you would give it a try. That's great! As long as you won't feel overworked by taking it on along with your marketing responsibilities, we feel certain that you can handle the acting role."

"I have a lot of energy, Jack. If you wouldn't mind, though, I'd like to be in on the auditioning for the male lead. Okay?"

"Of course, we want you there since you will be working with him and we'll need good chemistry between you two." Jack, never one for small talk, then got up and said, "I'm glad that we got that settled. You can go back to your work. Thanks, Nikki."

As soon as John publicized the auditions, applications began pouring in. He scheduled four auditions for the same date, so comparisons could be fresh in their minds. Ted was there to accompany the singers with whatever song they chose to sing for their tryout.

The first singer had a good background in the field. He had sung in three musicals – two in small parts and one as the lead. Even so, he appeared nervous and stiff as he sang "What Kind of Fool Am I" in a pleasing tenor voice. Ted, Jack, John, Roxy, and Nikki all felt he might be able to pull it off with training.

Next was Jason, a nice-looking young man who had majored in music in college and had been in two musicals as the leading man. He picked "All I Ask of You" from *Phantom of the Opera*, which brought a smile to Nikki's face. He had only sung a line when they were all blown away by his baritone voice. They were nodding to each other with raised eyebrows that said, "This guy is perfect." When he had finished singing, Jason sat down to listen to the last two auditions.

The next two were both good, but the judges had already picked Jason in their minds. John thanked them all and asked Jason to stay behind for a while. Jason was self-assured without being egotistic. He was twenty-four years old, average size, with chestnut-colored hair that was a bit unruly and thick. His blue eyes sparkled as he came up to the five judges.

John introduced him to each one, and when he came to Nikki, John told Jason that she would be the lead playing opposite him. Jason surprised himself when he exclaimed, "Sweet!" They all laughed and the ice was broken. Nikki felt that she was going to enjoy working with this personable young man.

Jason Yearal was from the Boston area but he hoped to rent a room in Maine while he worked on the musical instead of commuting from his old apartment that he shared with two other recently graduated music majors. Jason said that all of them used the one piano that was in the apartment, which made it quite difficult to schedule time to practice. He asked

John if he could use the music hall piano to practice his part. Not only did John agree to that arrangement, but he also offered him a room at the inn at a below average price. John wasn't about to lose this find. Already John was picturing the crowd that these two great voices would attract. Dollar signs were dancing in his head.

Jack, being the producer, had some contracts ready to have Jason read and sign. He also explained to Jason that he'd be on salary all the while he was working on the musical, so he was not to worry about his room and board expenses. Jason was thrilled with the arrangements, especially when he heard that Nikki worked at the inn weekends. He was anxious to get to know her better.

Once the audition was over, they all went to the inn for dinner. Jason was asked to join them at their table and he found that he fit as if he had known them all before. He said that he had to give his notice before he could move to the inn. In the meantime, he would commute so that they could get started right away. That suited everyone just fine.

After dinner, Jason made a point of going up to Nikki. She was in no hurry to leave the inn so they both went on the porch and sat in the wicker rockers for a while.

"So you're to be my leading lady, Nikki! How lucky can a guy get?"

"It should be fun, Jason. Ted is wonderful to work with and they are trying to find a good director." She nodded and said, "That's quite the voice you have there, Jason! We were all very impressed!"

"Thanks. I have yet to hear you sing. I understand that you have a following here at the inn. That tells me I have something to look forward to when I finally hear you perform."

They talked about college and briefly about their lives. Finally, Nikki said that she was heading home. Jason had to get back to his apartment but was planning on coming back up tomorrow. Both parted with great hopes for a promising future.

The next day, the two met at the inn. Because Ted was going to be busy at the lounge in the afternoon, Nikki suggested they go to her house, where Eileen would welcome having them practice while she was painting. She explained to Jason that although they didn't have a piano, her guitar would work out well enough.

"So you play the guitar, Nikki! That's cool!"

"I like to accompany myself with it and sometimes I think that it comes together better than with a piano."

"Yeah, I know what you mean. I play a little myself." He took out the music and said, "I spent last night running over the music and I like it a lot. The harmony is unusual and that will give a contemporary twist to our parts. The music world always welcomes fresh ideas."

"Yes, I think so too. That's the result of Ted's working with Roxy. Those two are able to come up with some unique ideas. As talented as Ted is, I think that he needs her to jazz it up at times."

Nikki got her guitar and they sat on the porch swing in comfort with lemonade drinks on the small table in front of them. They worked line by line of each song until they no longer needed to look at the music. They were unaware of the passing hours until Eileen told them that she had supper ready for them. She insisted that Jason stay and he didn't try to argue.

After eating, he looked at Eileen and said, "Have you any idea of how long it has been since I had a homemade meal this good? How do you stay so slim, Nikki?"

"Portions, Jason, small portions. We should meet with Ted tomorrow morning to have him check out what we have done. We don't want to get off on the wrong track. He knows exactly how he wants us to sing his songs. I'll phone you in the morning when I know what time Ted will meet us at the music hall."

"Sounds good to me." When they reached his car, he said, "It was nice working with you, Nikki. And to think I am being paid for this! How great is that?" He drove off leaving Nikki agreeing with his assessment.

In the meantime, Eric was spending a lot of time revising his novel into a script. He had to make sure that the words flowed nicely into the song that would follow. He had never done anything like that before and found it challenging. Eric always made sure that he had enough time set aside to be with Eileen. That was the best part of his day in his opinion. Eileen looked forward to reading his progress and they both found it helpful to take the lead roles and try them out. He appreciated Eileen's suggestions and together they polished up parts before showing them to Jack, John, Nikki, and Jason. Once they approved, Ted and Roxy had the final say as to how the script tied in with their music. And so the musical became a team effort which spurred them on.

The first act had to be perfect before the second one was even looked at. Nikki and Jason took their copies and decided to practice at the beach. When they got to the bench, Nikki explained to Jason the story behind this particular bench.

Nikki explained. "Eric was sitting here on this very bench when Mom was done with her shore walk. She had to come up to the bench because her sneakers were left beside it. If she hadn't left them there, she never would have met him and their romance never would have happened. So you see, they consider this bench their own special bench."

Jason was impressed with how fate touched people's lives and here was another example. "That's quite a story!"

Nikki had to smile. "Let's start going over the first page, Jason, to get a feel for it."

The hours passed quickly and they felt they accomplished more than they had expected to get done at the beach. They ended up going for a short walk which turned into a long walk as they discovered how comfortable they were together. Nikki told him he'd be welcome if he wanted to come to her house for another of Eileen's dinners. Not wanting to make a pest of himself, he reluctantly declined.

When Nikki arrived home, Eileen had a pot roast with lots of vegetables and thick gravy, all waiting for her daughter to join her for dinner. As Nikki walked in, she took a deep breath to take in the alluring aroma.

"So how are you and Jason coming along with the musical?"

"Oh, Mom, he's so easy to work with! We have so much in common and he has a great sense of humor, too."

"It seems he's made a big impression on you, Nikki."

"Yeah, you're right. And did you notice that he has a very nice speaking voice? I think that will be a big asset when we do this play. He is a fast learner, too. We tested each other and he could remember his lines without any trouble."

As the weeks passed by, the rehearsals became more and more polished. Jason and Nikki played the role of lovers so believably that it wasn't surprising when they announced that they were a couple. It made the director's job much easier. At the rate everything was progressing, they all felt they could set the opening date for early spring. John had such faith that it would succeed that he left a large slot open for an extended month. May and June would be the start of the season for vacationers to the region. And, of course, word of mouth would help bring the buses from outside areas. Jack spread the word to his New York friends that he would supply free tickets to any of the entertainment writers who would like to check out his musical. Meanwhile, Eileen's friend Renée was already busy letting people know about the original musical with the talented new singers. Interest was spreading and the inn was already receiving reservations for early vacationers.

With the arrival of winter, the music hall shut down except for the occasional rehearsal and small changes to the story line. In April, the hall was opened daily for serious rehearsals to meet the May opening plans. Costumes were being redesigned for everyone's approval. Set designers were busy following Nikki's instructions for each scene. The orchestra now playing at rehearsals gave an emotional impact to the songs, which impressed the whole group. Nikki no longer worried about her acting, which resulted in her completely immersing herself in her stage character, Jennifer.

Opening night arrived with a sold-out audience and the first row occupied by Eileen, Eric, John, Jack, Anne, Roxy, and Ted, all excitedly waiting for the curtain to open. The lights dimmed and the orchestra launched into an overture of the beautiful songs. Then the curtain drew back to reveal a country setting with Jason on a hillside with his backpack where he stopped to rest on a rock. His character, Adam, used sweeping gestures as he sang of how he was drawn to the beauty of nature and his passion for hiking and exploring.

When he finished his song, the audience stopped the show as they clapped in appreciation of Jason's great voice and the new song. Soon afterwards, Nikki arrived, as Jennifer, with a basket of wildflowers. They met and conversed and then it was Jennifer's time to sing about gathering these flowers of the hill to raise her spirits. As she sang her song, Nikki performed a graceful dance she had choreographed herself. The audience was delighted and showed it with another round of applause.

The show continued on smoothly until intermission, when the actors assessed how the play was coming together so far. They all agreed that it was better than they dared to hope for. The second half was even better as their confidence built with each act. The final curtain call went on and on as the audience refused to stop applauding. Jack came on stage when they called for the producer. It was then that Jack silenced the crowd to explain how this musical was a group effort by his friends. He talked about the great book that Eric had written and Eileen's influence on Eric and also how Ted and Roxy teamed to match the music to the play. He also let the audience in on a secret when he told them that Jason and Nikki were dating in their personal lives, just as they were in the play. This brought on more clapping in approval.

Everyone left that night with smiles on their faces and songs in their heads. The critics wrote wonderful reviews praising this group of novices that put on a hit musical. Reservations poured in for both the play and the inn. John couldn't have been happier. He spent hours adding up expenses and income. They were going to come out way ahead by the time the play had run its course.

A week later, when Eileen went to the beach, she saw Eric waiting for her. She took off her sneakers and placed them in their usual spot. Since it was a hot day, she decided that a jacket wasn't needed so she left it on the bench. As they started for their walk, Eric paused and said, "You know, I think I'll leave my jacket behind, too. Be right back."

Eric carefully slipped a small box shaped like the Tavern on the Green restaurant, into her sneaker.

After a short walk, they returned to the bench, where Eileen reached for her sneakers and discovered the box. While she opened it, Eric dropped down on one knee and proposed. She accepted with joy and raved about the engagement ring he had chosen, which had a large diamond with an emerald on each side. Eileen handed him the ring to place on her finger, leaving them with thoughts for a bright future as husband and wife.

About the Author

Dolores Yergeau has gone from having her short story published in *The Book of Knowledge* at the age of fifteen, to having her first novel published as a great-grandmother of ten. She has written and illustrated booklets for her great-grandkids where they were the central characters. Dolores hopes to pass on her love of storytelling.

CPSIA information can be obtained
at www.ICGtesting.com
Printed in the USA
FFHW020754021219
56478790-62283FF